# BY
# MY OWN
# BETRAYAL

# PRAISE FOR
# BY MY OWN BETRAYAL

"Action-packed and Gospel-centered, *By My Own Betrayal* is a heart-pounding story, reminiscent of Frank Peretti's Veritas Project series, that will enthrall Christian teens and inspire them to follow Jesus and leave everything else behind, no matter the cost."

- Erin Phillips, author of
*A Crown of Chains*

"Entering the sphere of Young Adult action spy novels comes the stunning debut by Cydnie Trenholm. Filled with themes of family, integrity, and choosing to believe the truth, this novel explores what it truly means to stand up for what you believe in, no matter what the cost. Through it all is wound the beautiful tale of perfect redemption found in Christ alone. Perfect for fans of Marvel and James Bond!"

- Cheyenne van Langevelde, author of
*Between Two Worlds* and
the *Princess of the Highlands Trilogy*

'Trenholm presents a fast, clever story that will leave its readers wanting more. Her well-crafted prose and deep characters are absolutely brilliant."

- Nathaniel Luscombe, author of
*The Ones with Gilded Bones*

"*By My Own Betrayal* is a fresh and unique take on the sacrifices God asks for in our lives. Trenholm — and God — take Sadie from darkness into light on this harrowing journey. From hired assassin to working with the FBI, Sadie places her life on the line for her newfound faith and hope. Trenholm paints an edge-of-your-seat picture of Sadie's life before and after encountering Jesus — and doesn't sugar coat the cost of accepting that incredible life."

- Sara Marlowe Jolene, author of
*The Seed of Euforemalta* and
*The Magenta Trilogy*

# BY
# MY OWN
# BETRAYAL

CYDNIE TRENHOLM

Published 2021 by:
Cydnie Trenholm Publishing
www.cydnietrenholm.com

Printed in Canada.

ISBN: 978-1-7773452-0-4


Scripture passages taken from *The Holy Bible —New King James Version*. © 1982 by Thomas Nelson Inc. Used by permission.

*By My Own Betrayal* is a work of fiction. Although the novel is set in real places, all characters and events are purely fictitious and are in no way based upon real persons, either living or dead.

To Grandma Harrison, who has never ceased
to inspire and encourage me in my writing
and my walk with Jesus
~ Philippians 4:13 ~

# CHAPTER ONE

You'd think that after all these years of working at this desk, the chair would've become more comfortable. At least I should have gotten used to it.

I wasn't so fortunate.

I rolled my shoulders and leaned into the desk—my desk. Two pages stared back at me, taunting with arrows and colours that organized my content flawlessly. Normally, such a spreadsheet of information and inferences would spark excitement throughout my body. Instead, the dread that captured my slim frame was a completely new sensation.

Nothing was wrong.

I leaned back and ran a hand through my long, black hair, distracting myself from work by studying the pink walls of my bedroom. My hideout. It was still filled with little-girl things— well, aside from the advanced chemistry and university-level political science textbooks on my shelf, or the handgun I had mounted on my wall for emergency purposes. Other than that, the room reeked of childlike wonder and excitement. A place where any problem could be fixed by simply thinking of something different.

I glanced back at the pages.

Distraction didn't work anymore.

I got up and opened the window. Despite its small size, it often made a world of difference, letting in more sunlight and fresh air than any other window in our mostly underground home.

I sat again in my uncomfortable chair, breathing deeply and eyeing my work as if a mere gaze could change the results. I checked my conclusion again.

"How could something be so right, yet so wrong?" I exhaled.

Gathering my pages, I abstained from pacing and headed downstairs. In the kitchen, my mother and older brother Dean were preparing a celebration meal. Shawn, my oldest brother, had the weapons from our last mission on the dinner table and was busy cleaning and inspecting them. Tyson, the youngest, was nowhere to be found, implying that he was stationed in front of his bedroom computer. Jonathan was also missing-in-action, but the deep bass of electronic music booming from the training room pinpointed his whereabouts.

"Where's Dad?" I asked Mom. She picked up a pan of uncooked lasagna. I opened the oven door.

"In his office. We'll be debriefing as soon as this is all cooking," Mom answered as she slid the pan in, then turned for another one.

As if on cue Tyson appeared, slipping through the kitchen into his place at the table while Shawn hauled his now-polished arsenal out of the adjoined dining room. He returned with Jonathan in tow, and I joined the rest of my family at the table, tucking my pages beneath its worn wooden surface. I heard the door to the lowest level of our underground home—Dad's office—shut, and the man emerged from around the corner. He sat at the head of the table, keeping his chin elevated and purposefully making eye contact with each of us.

"Let's talk about today," Dad said, opening our meeting. "Any general thoughts?"

Dean smirked. "Well, I don't think Mr. Jameson will be elected this year."

A subtle chuckle slipped between my father and brothers. "Well, the advancements in health care do make our job a bit tricky…" Dad grinned. "But our shot will have bypassed that."

Mom rolled her eyes. "Anything else?" she asked. We had a narrow window of time before melted cheese would waft to our noses and end focused discussion.

My stomach firmly reminded me of my concerns. I laid my papers on the table and asked, "Did today seem off to anyone?"

"Off?" Dad inquired.

"Yeah. Like we missed something," I elaborated slightly.

A circle of noes met my question.

Shawn spoke: "We may be conducting a few more…" he fought for the word, "risky jobs, but that doesn't mean we're being careless, Sadie."

Dean countered, "And you, Ms. Seamstress, called the shot. How 'off' could it be?"

As if I hadn't thought about that. As if calling the shot was my choice.

Mom leaned into the conversation. Before she could utter a word, Dad pressed: "What exactly is your concern?"

I flipped the pages onto my lap, concealing the bright ink. "It was just a question. If I'm the only one who thought that way, then obviously it's fine. Proceed."

Dad furrowed his brow, and I didn't have to look at Mom to know that she was analyzing my body language for any telltale signs of what was really going on. After a moment, Dad redirected the meeting back to the actual assassination of Mr. Ron Jameson, reviewing the facts and the options for the next job to keep us all safer and make the kill shot surer. With one more glance at my papers, I pushed away whatever "off" feeling I had. It wasn't backed by fact or logic, so it was banished.

At least, that's what I told myself.

~~

"Use the common to hide the uncommon." These were the words penned on the first page of my great-grandmother's journal. The journal itself was full of poems she'd written. To the average person, these poems seemed like beautiful pieces about falling in love and the beauty of nature. To our family, they were heavily enriched with codes and plans for different operations, carried by a precise handwriting that was second-to-none.

In other words, my great-grandmother knew what she was doing. She was the queen of her craft, executing relentless perfection in her work. Her words and teachings held the families of her children and her grandchildren together and spurred us all to perform more effectively. That made her journal my most treasured book in the entire house.

My reading was interrupted by my father's booming voice echoing through the halls. I cocked an eyebrow, placed the journal gently on the bed, and hurried downstairs to the main level of our home, stopping short of the last step.

I peeked around the wall that separated the dining room from the staircase. Dad had a pen and pad in his hand and an ear glued to the old-fashioned phone that was tethered to the wall. This phone was the epitome of our clandestine lifestyle: a secret agreement with a company, a hidden line, and a number that only previous contacts knew and could pass on.

I leaned from my post in the hallway to catch a glance at Dad's notes. I ran back up the stairs, popping my head into Tyson and Shawn's shared room.

"Guys, we have another job," I stated. Their eyes grew wide.

"Where?" Tyson asked.

"When?" Shawn responded at the same time.

I smiled. "Come find out."

Within a matter of minutes, the Black family had assembled around the dining room table to discuss our next source of employment.

"What are we looking at?" Shawn asked, stealing the words from between my lips.

Dad stood at the end of the table, laying his sheet of paper in front of us. "Our target is Mr. Nathan Raleigh, CEO of Raleigh Technologies. His office and home are out-of-state. We'll have to travel light. Deadline is three weeks from today."

I smirked as a wave of adrenaline surged throughout the room.

Dad turned to Mom. "Honey, I need you on the inside. I don't know how, but get there." He didn't even glance at his notes as he shifted his attention to the rest of us. "Tyson, I want you to hack into Raleigh's personal and office computers. Find out his schedule as well as his security measures. Jonathan, prep the van for the road and for blending in. Dean, map out clear entrance and exit strategies for the office and house. Prep a backup plan and meeting place. Shawn, work with Tyson and Sadie to figure out what supplies we'll use and where we'll be using them. Sadie, you make sure it looks like nothing happens. I'll be ensuring that something does."

"Dad, what's the motivation behind this client?" I asked, clicking my pen against the table.

"Part revenge, part promotion. The entire business shifts when the CEO resigns, let alone when he dies suddenly."

"Bullet, poison, or accident?" I asked.

Dad shrugged while the corners of his lips lifted smugly. "Surprise me," he said, scanning the table once more. "We report back in two days. Dismissed."

Just as quickly as we had gathered, each Black retreated to complete his or her assigned task. Time was our only true enemy, and it had given us less than a month to attain perfection.

# CHAPTER TWO

My siblings and I only interacted over quick coffee breaks and folder exchanges for the next two days. Reports, images, and sketches adorned my bedroom walls. One consolidated list, summing up the key points from loads of intel we had collected, sat on my desk:

*Home: Suburban. 5032 Ash Street Northwest*

*Work: Raleigh Technologies corporate building. Downtown.*

*Health: Excellent. Consistent medical checkups and physicals to back it up. Heart attack or other sudden illness is unlikely.*

*Habits: Has a cable TV subscription and a surprising amount of unscheduled time.*

*Security: Raleigh Technologies corporate building has standard security procedures, including cameras and security personnel. Home security details unknown.*

I dropped my head to the desk. Thirty-six hours of this had gnawed considerably at my patience and enthusiasm for the job. Having little to show for it only made the situation worse.

My small fingers flipped through a few more papers. One confirmed that Mom had wiggled her way into a substitute janitorial position at Raleigh's office, giving her access to nearly the whole building if needed. Another page held three potential escape plans from both the office and house, and a neon green sticky note told me that Jonathan had finished necessary maintenance on the van. Nothing mentioned any back roads that the target would be driving or any gardening hobbies that would bring the target outside, and Raleigh had no history as a late-night partier.

Tyson poked his head through the doorway. "Sadie, I have more security details."

My head sprung up. "Let me see!" I blurted, ripping Tyson's work from his hands. "How tight are we?"

"Well," Tyson flipped into a Russian accent, "his house has a high number of tracking cameras. If something moves, they will follow it. They're not hard to hack, though."

"For you, anyway," I said as I playfully rolled my eyes. Despite our family's rich Italian heritage, the Russian accent was his default.

"Well, it would be easier if we had decent equipment." Tyson tilted his head. "But yes. Not hard for me." The Russian accent stayed strong. He, too, must have felt the intense monotony of the last couple of days.

"Any human guards? Dogs?" I asked.

"He has three armed guards on patrol all the time, but their firearm training is hardly exemplary." He dropped the accent. "There is also a housekeeper."

"Where are the guards positioned?" I asked, pressing for the elusive piece of data that would solidify a foolproof plan.

"One on the exterior perimeters, one watching the camera feeds, and one within Raleigh's reach most of the time."

"Hmm…" I flicked through Tyson's research. An aerial map of the target's home property stared back at me. "Motion sensors other than the cameras?"

Tyson flipped the map in my hands to a diagram, revealing the placement and ranges of all the motion sensors. "Based on what I'm seeing, we can snipe it," Tyson concluded.

"But then we have to frame someone else for the shot to keep our client in the clear." I shook my head. "Not enough time."

"You doubt my ability?" Tyson feigned a hurt voice.

"No." I dropped Tyson's information, grabbing and thumbing through my paperwork again. An excited grin pushed against my cheekbones. "It's an inside job, anyway." I stopped to look back at my little brother. "How many people are in the house during the day?"

"The housekeeper and a single guard."

Perfect.

~~

I stepped into Dad's office. "Dad…so, after considering the options, I was thinking—"

"Sounds good, Sadie," Dad interrupted, eyes still glued to the papers on his desk.

I blinked. "I didn't even tell you my plan," I said.

"Don't need to. Because if you're my daughter," Dad began, "and you think anything like me, you will have determined that 'suicide' would keep our identity safe as well as keeping the job clean." Dad slid a piece of paper across his desk. "Here's how we're going to do it."

I wasn't sure if I was flattered, offended, or simply stunned. "So why have me working on a plan if you have one finished already?"

Dad paused his work and turned toward me. "I'm doing what your grandfather did with me, and what his mother did with him. I'm training you. The only way to get better," he explained, eyes now back on his desk, "is to do it. You, Sadie, are more than capable, so I train you." I watched his hands follow the lines of information on the pages in front of him.

I gingerly picked up the paperwork and began to scan it.

Dad continued. "Memorize the plan and the backup. You will ensure that it all goes the way it should."

"Yes, sir." I left his office, strode up the stairs and down the hall, and slid into my desk chair. I finished reading.

In a matter of seconds I was back in Dad's office.

"What is this?" I demanded, planting my feet firmly and waving his so-called training exercise.

"The plan." Dad seemed smug.

"Yeah, and the part where I'm the one with the gun?" That wasn't my job. I liked my job.

"You're the smallest," Dad responded. I'd never truly been happy with the fact that I was a head shorter than my brothers. Now, that unhappiness multiplied.

I mentally pointed out that our code names—Archer and Seamstress—were chosen for good reasons.

Finality rested on his face. There was no moving him.

I sighed and headed back up to my room, taking in the decades of assassins that lined our walls, each preserved in paint and framed ornately. Small, coded poems, used before the technology of comms units began, were posted on the wall, breaking up the individual portraits. My great-grandmother's portrait, in my opinion, was the most striking. Maybe it was the way the artist had accented her toned muscles underneath her tight, crimson sleeves, or maybe it was how Grandma's jawline was so strong yet charmingly feminine. Most likely, it was the simple reality that the woman in the portrait reminded me of the woman in the mirror. Although every member of my family held a stark resemblance, none in my generation shared my jet-black hair. Grandma did. Even through the painting, her sapphire eyes shot through mine, cutting me to the core. If I had to share my appearance with anyone, I was glad it was her.

I skimmed Dad's plan one more time and looked back at my great-grandma, the pinnacle of unshakable determination and refined confidence. A renewed sense of privilege and earnest duty swelled throughout my body.

The job I would be doing next was exactly her craft. I would do it well.

# CHAPTER THREE

Time was truly my enemy. Not only in terms of limited time to prepare for a job, but also in the nine-hour drive to complete that job. Now, some might believe driving to be the tranquil calm before a storm, but the fact that our technology hardware occupied more space in our crowded van than my family did would vouch otherwise.

I closed my eyes. That nasty "off" feeling from our last mission had returned, adding to the mental cacophony of logic and emotions while sending the butterflies in my stomach on a crash course. The low rumble of the van and the puns coming from the backseat, however annoying they seemed, did little in drowning out the psychological noise.

Fifteen minutes until destination.

Mom turned to face me from the passenger seat. "You'll be fine, hun."

Did I look that nervous?

Dad gave a recap of the operation. Tyson had already hacked the security system and the house's electronic features, causing a need for the "Wayne's Furnace Installation and Repair" company to act on their warranty and diagnose the issues behind a finicky furnace. We also had a running visual of all that went on in the Raleigh household.

Tyson winced as the van bounced off the curb to a stop in front of the Raleigh Technologies corporate headquarters. Mom slipped out of the vehicle, giving me a confident smile as she left. As Dean drove away, Jonathan wedged himself into the now-empty passenger seat, ready for the next stage of the plan. So far it had been an uneventful trip.

That's the way we liked it.

Shawn and Dad hopped out of the van as we turned the corner into Raleigh's driveway. Though it was short, the wall of evergreens on either side of the lane's entrance gave the visual protection that they'd need to see without being seen. Their departure resulted in some extra interior space, so Tyson slipped amid the maze of computers, cables, and wires installed in the back of the van. I crawled around our technical genius to reach my own piece of equipment for this job: a hefty metal toolbox.

Dean rolled to a stop at the front door, cueing he and Jonathan to jump out in their matching blue repairman's coveralls. Meanwhile, I began the task of squishing myself into the rather large, empty (but still highly confining) toolbox.

"So that's why we keep you around," Tyson teased as I shoved my lower half into the box, folding my torso, arms, and head tightly over top. I shot a glare back at him before he closed the lid, surrounding my body with a thin layer of darkness.

"Good afternoon," Dean's charm oozed from my earpiece. "We're here to fix your furnace."

"Keep it cool, Lightning." Dad chided. I wasn't the only one put in a different position for this job.

"Oh, come in!" I heard a soft voice say. I assumed that to be the housekeeper. The door creaked and shut.

More dialogue was heard. They discussed the problem and the location, as well as the solution.

"I have just the part for that, ma'am," Dean continued. "We'll go grab it from the van."

"Showtime." Tyson's body shifted to the very back of the van. I counted the heavy footsteps from the front door. The van door rolled open.

"You'd better not drop me," I hissed as they placed the toolbox on the ground and wheeled it into the house and through the hall—one left, two rights. Tools clunked and banged as my two brothers "fixed" the furnace.

"CPU, am I clear?" I breathed, squeezing the words from my condensed mouth space. It was during moments like these that I was glad we'd shortened Tyson's code name from "Computer" to "CPU." The simplicity of sounds made all the difference.

"Security out of premise. Go ahead," Tyson responded through comms from the van. His voice was followed by the sweet sound of my brother unclasping the lid. Dean popped the top of the toolbox open and pulled me out. I'm sure that he, too, wanted to make some wisecrack about my smallness and being a truly "little" sister, but we simply nodded as I turned for the hallway.

"Left," Tyson commanded. His directions led me safely to the target's home office.

I slowly pushed the door closed behind me, turning the doorknob until it would silently re-engage. My boots sank into the carpeted floor as I stepped toward the window, while my hand flicked a knife by my side. Its blade sliced along the edges of the screen, creating my final escape route.

"Seamstress, the safe is just to your left," Tyson directed. I recognized the space from the blueprints, but the safe was entirely concealed by outdated wood panelling and paint, leaving only what appeared to be a new thermostat as an access point. "It will be opening in three…two…one." The safe clicked open, revealing the shiny interior of the next metal box that would become my hideout until the target came home.

I thrust my body past full envelopes and packages of what I assumed to be cash, crawling into yet one more tight space. Having wiggled into a semi-comfortable spot, I whispered, "Seamstress is in position."

Gears pulled the safe door closed beside me. "And now… she's locked in," Tyson confirmed.

"Okay boys, let's wrap this up," Dad said.

I could hear the satisfaction in Tyson's voice as he proceeded to wirelessly "fix" the furnace malfunction that he'd caused earlier in the week from the convenience of his keyboard. "Problem solved, Thunder and Lightning. Clear to leave premise."

Sighs of relief from Dean and Jonathan came through the comms unit as they exited the house. All the pieces were in place; now we just had to wait.

So I waited, and I squirmed.

"Question: how am I supposed to make the kill shot if my legs and arms are numb?" I asked.

"Relax, hun." Mom's voice came through the earpiece. The range on these comms units was incredible. "The target just left the office. You have maybe fifteen minutes left at the most.”

So I waited, and I continued to squirm. Moving slightly, something gave way under my left elbow.

Now, I know that assassins don’t snoop, at least no more than necessary. We were better than that. I did not need to push harder to see why that gave way. But in fact, I should’ve been more concerned about the possibility that someone had put a sensor inside the safe.

“CPU, there is no security in my position, correct?” Okay, I was slightly concerned.

“None,” Tyson confirmed without hesitation. “Why?”

“Curiosity,” I responded, and my elbow once again shifted. I heard a pop as a small door opened.

My pocket flashlight clicked beside me.

Was this completely against protocol? Yes.

However, a secret door within an already secure, hidden safe was odd to say the least. As the Seamstress, it was practically my protocol to investigate—or so I told myself.

I peeked. The small door opened into a larger, much more “Sadie-sized” safe. It was full of papers, artifacts, and more money. My flashlight beam shone on an agreement for a cross-country shipment of “goods,” confirming that the target was less than an honest businessman. He was like us—taking life to gain a profit. The difference was that the life he took remained alive.

“Target has driven onto premise,” Dad said.

I shoved the document back on the pile and carefully closed the small door.

“Target is approaching the front door,” Shawn continued the narrative.

"I have visual," Tyson said. "Target has a briefcase in hand and is heading to the office." I touched the black 9 mm handgun strapped to my right hip, listening. "Target is opening the door." I breathed deeply as Tyson updated: "And…target is in the office."

"Don't be too quick. Give him time to settle in," Dad said firmly. "Keep tabs on the security."

Everything was in place. The true quiet before the storm had begun. For a moment, time was on our side.

"Okay, Seamstress, the target is on the far right of his desk and sitting in his chair. I'm opening the door in three…two…ONE." The door clicked. I pushed. My boots hit the floor and I turned. Raleigh looked up from his desk. My gloved hand fell in line with the target's chest. Fear plastered Raleigh's face. I tapped the trigger.

Raleigh's face reflected my own shock.

Nothing came from the barrel.

"Shoot!" Tyson yelled.

The target ducked.

I ran toward him and jumped, carrying the momentum across his desk. I aimed and fired again.

A bullet penetrated his skull. The target's body fell limply onto the carpet. His hand had been in a drawer, pulling out his own (and might I add expensive) pistol.

Talk about paranoid.

I quickly wrapped my arms around the target's chest and heaved him up into his desk chair. Leaving my own weapon in his hand, I strapped the gun from his drawer to my side.

"Security heard the shot and is headed your way. Maybe ten seconds," Tyson warned calmly.

Shawn updated: "Outside front window is clear." I moved to the window. Heavy footsteps shook the walls. I crawled through the opening, checking to make sure that the screen appeared unaltered. My feet and legs pushed against the building, propelling myself farther away from my first kill and flinging my body into a tight backflip—straight into some raspberry bushes.

"Ach," I spat, twisting through and out of the tall branches. Blood dripped from the scratches on my face.

"Should've jumped farther," Shawn advised sarcastically through the comms unit.

I scowled. I had barely pulled myself out of the thorny shrubbery when sirens pierced the air.

"Guys…" Shawn's voice shook slightly.

"There must be a secondary security system," Tyson said, sounding scrambled. "Get out of there now!"

I bolted for the evergreens. The branches shook as Shawn and Dad shimmied down them.

"Over there!" yelled a gruff voice. I turned to see a guard pointing at me, with another one close behind. Both were armed.

"Seamstress will meet you at the backup meeting place," I said as I dashed down the lane, away from the trees and away from the van.

I hit the open suburban street and steered hard right. A bullet sliced through the air.

I swerved, turning briefly to fire back.

Those guards were much too close for comfort.

My arms and legs pumped in time with my heart, forcing me toward the centre of the city. The footsteps behind me grew louder, while my ears buzzed with the urgent voices of my family. I pushed harder, slipping into an alley. The guards maintained close pursuit. Another shot fired from behind. I slid around a corner, crouching to aim again.

The alley echoed with the shot, followed by another bullet smashing into the brick wall beside me.

I bolted onto a main road, hoping for some pedestrian cover.

Nothing.

My calves burned and my lungs gasped. Two more gunshots whizzed by. I whipped my hand back to return fire.

The gun only clicked.

Great.

I flung the empty weapon at my pursuers as I veered right. Anxiety gripped my chest, begging for an even greater adrenaline rush.

Another right turn revealed sanctuary: someone had left a front door open a crack.

Glancing over my shoulder, I yanked open the door and bolted inside, pulling it closed behind me.

Unsure of the type of building I'd entered, I rushed to where I heard voices. My pace slowed just before a set of double doors, trying to bring my heart rate down with my speed. I glanced to where blood-splattered gloves had grasped a lethal weapon and a dead body. It only took 7.5 seconds to rip off my soiled gloves and jacket and wipe off my scratched face.

Folding my incriminating holster inside the clothing that I'd removed, I pushed against the door.

Here, a large room with lots of people offered shelter. They were organized into theatre-style rows, all facing away from me. I slipped into a row where there was no direct line of sight to the door I'd just entered. If they followed me this far, and I couldn't see the door, the guards likely wouldn't see me, either.

Two little girls—one freckled and strawberry blonde, the other with dark skin and tightly braided hair—smiled innocently at me as their peers and others old enough to be their parents and grandparents sang in harmony around us. Even the children in the group seemed to know all the words by heart, while a few adults needed prompting from the large screen at the front of the room. I tried to mouth the words to hide my heavy panting.

I was only semi-successful.

"Seamstress, where are you?" Dad's voice echoed loudly in my ear. I could only assume that this was a church. Believe it or not, this was not the place where a family of assassins had planned to stage a rendezvous.

"Improvising. Will keep you posted," I whispered.

"You may be seated." A man's voice boomed across the room.

"Seamstress out." I pulled the earpiece from my ear, catching the sideways glance of an elderly gentleman down the row. I was already dressed head-to-toe in black carrying a carefully folded blood-stained jacket; I didn't need help to look suspicious.

Now that the group was seated, I could register my location. There were beige walls decorated with vines of artificial autumn leaves, and bold "Jesus is Lord" banners rose from a floor lined with chairs. The smell of perfume clung to the air, matching the dressed-up appearance of those in attendance. At the front of the room, a rough, wooden cross was positioned to the right of the screen, looking over a humble podium. An older man in a bright-blue dress shirt and light grey suit approached the platform.

My leg muscles continued to burn, and a stitch developed in my right side. I mentally mapped how I had arrived in a church—at least I attempted to. Adrenaline blended the streets and alleys of my high-speed escape route into one.

Not a comforting thought.

I checked my watch. Waiting the extra five minutes to ensure that the guards had cleared the area dragged into an eternity.

Finally, I slipped out of the row, heading for the back of the room and the nearest exit.

"What are you doing?" resonated throughout the small auditorium. My fingertips rested on the push bar of the door. I cautiously turned my head, hearing the speaker continue his spiel.

"What are *we* doing? Christ can free us from our guilt, our shame, our emptiness, but how many times do we believe the lie that we can free ourselves? Death itself has no power over Jesus, yet…"

My fingers retracted out of curiosity.

Religion had not been a prominent study in my youth, but I knew that my career choice was deemed wrong by just about everyone. I leaned against the door frame, listening and trying to pick apart his argument and his reasoning. It all sounded crazy, and yet a thread of appeal weaved itself through the words he spoke.

The presenter's "Amen" broke my trance. With the crowd likely leaving right away, I could use them as additional cover to manoeuvre back to my family.

"Hello there!" A deep, animated voice reached out from behind me, grabbing my attention in a way I couldn't dismiss despite the ridiculously short distance that lay between me and the door. Turning, I froze. The speaker's brown eyes contained genuine joy as he said, "I'm glad to see you stayed, Miss—"

Hesitation gripped my throat. The door posed a clear image in my mind.

"Sadie," I answered. He proceeded to introduce himself as Pastor Ben and the woman beside him as his wife Katherine.

"What brings you here this morning?" Pastor Ben asked.

Neither "an assassination job" nor "two goons with guns" seemed like an appropriate answer, so I shrugged and suggested, "Fate?"

The job must have still been prominently on my mind, as "Fate" was Mom's code name.

He chuckled. "I see. Did you have any questions or anything we could help you with?"

Questions? Yes. Time? No.

"Actually, I do, but…" I trailed off, making eye contact with Katherine. Her eyes shone like stars in the sky, reaching out to the darkness of Earth.

I couldn't say another word.

Katherine took the opportunity. "Perhaps," she spoke softly, "I can put on a pot of coffee and we can try to help you in the study."

The comms unit sat heavy in my pocket. I *really* couldn't stay.

"Does that work for you, Sadie?" Pastor Ben asked.

Then again, further time spent here could only help secure my safe departure. Who would expect an assassin to stay after the church service?

The feeling in my gut crept up my spine, contributing its own insistent opinion to my mental debate.

I nodded in consent.

The couple guided me into a room close to the front of the church and motioned for me to sit. Bookshelves lined the walls, full of study books, commentaries, and volumes on what I assumed to be different aspects of religion: Psalms, Gospels, history, etc. A desk sat in the middle of the room, where a plaque bore the inscription, "Pastor Benjamin Monroe." The pastor pulled a leather-bound book from one shelf and a chair from the wall beside it. He moved another chair for his wife and sat across from me, away from the desk. Katherine returned with the coffee, and we began our conversation.

The pastor opened the worn book, which he called his Bible, and told me about the creation of the world, answering my questions as we went along. He told me briefly of how the first man and woman ever to walk the earth rejected their Creator and "sinned," and that death is the just consequence of sin. He explained that God sent His Son Jesus Christ to die and take the penalty of sin and save humanity from death, and that Jesus rose from the dead to give us a new life in Him.

It was a lot to take in.

"If this is true, why isn't everyone saved?" I questioned.

"Just like with Adam and Eve, God gives us the choice," Pastor Ben said.

Katherine added, "He gives it as a gift. Romans 6:23 says, 'For the wages of sin is death, but the gift of God is eternal life through Christ Jesus our Lord.' It's for anyone who accepts it."

The couple showed me a few more Bible passages. I was speechless. My "off" feeling ran rampant. My palms grew sweaty. My shoulders tensed. Everything in me wanted to run, knowing this Christian-thing could ruin my life.

But at the same time, everything in me knew that running was pointless. Regardless of my decision, my life would never be the same.

The "off" feeling and the terror of this morning burst from my body as tears and sobs, despite my best effort to keep them away. My body trembled as my head fell into my hands. Katherine moved her chair beside mine and placed her hand on my shoulder.

"Sadie," the pastor spoke gently. He didn't reprimand me for my tears. I looked at him. "Can we pray for you?" he asked.

I couldn't answer. My desires must have been visible, however, because the pastor also placed his hand on my shoulder. He bowed his head and began praying: "Dear Heavenly Father, You love us so much. I bring Sadie before You, Lord. You know her and love her so much. Lord, I don't know what she is going through, but I pray for Your will to be done, and that You would calm her heart. We thank you for Sadie, Lord God. Amen."

"Can I pray?" I uttered, taken back at the brokenness of my voice and the repercussions of such a question. My inner assassin screamed of devastation—not because of the lack of logic that this decision brought, but because it *was* logical. It fit with everything that I had been living. I was guilty. I was broken. I needed fixing. The payment for being fixed was my life, and the cost of being broken was death. Life seemed like a good option, and I wasn't going to chance the other option—not in my line of work.

The couple bowed their heads once more. "Dear God," I started, following how they'd prayed, "I really don't know about this. I have never known there to be anyone that could save me like You supposedly do. But I'm willing to give this a go. I know it won't be easy, but I'm deciding to believe in You and receive Your gift. Thanks for this."

The pastor and his wife finished my prayer with an "Amen."

My world fell silent. Tension fled my body, leaving it limp yet wonderfully light. I quickly inventoried my thoughts and emotions.

The "off" feeling had completely disappeared.

The couple looked up, taking in the new person sitting across from them. Tears clung to their eyes.

"Welcome to the family," Katherine told me, squeezing my shoulder slightly.

Family.

I immediately wiped away my tears. "I have to go," I declared quickly.

Pastor Ben's eyebrows leapt in surprise. "Oh, of course. Will you be back?" he asked.

"I live out of town," I responded. I fished through my pockets. Where did my comms unit go?

"Oh." Surprise and concern collided on his facial features.

"Let's give her a card, Ben," Katherine said. "Then she can reach us if needed." They both moved to grab a card with the pastor's personal contact information. I felt the comms unit deep in my pocket and clutched it. The couple located the card and handed it to me.

"I can't make any promises," I said, taking the card with my other hand. They surely had figured out that I lived in a closed community, so to speak.

Pastor Ben brought his hand to his chin and smiled. "I'll give you something better," he said, slipping behind his desk. A brand-new Bible appeared and made its way into my hands. I let go of my comms unit.

"I won't be able to return this," I said, shaking my head.

"It's a gift," Pastor Ben assured me. My finger traced the gold lettering on the cover.

"Thank you."

With that, I was off. It had nearly been three hours since I'd arrived in the church. I stuffed the Bible in my still-folded jacket and pulled the comms unit from my pocket, placing it in my ear.

"Seamstress is safe and back online. Anyone there?" I queried as I stepped onto the sidewalk. I still watched for the security guards from Raleigh's house.

Silence buzzed in my ear.

"Seamstress is back and is coming your direction. Do you copy?"

The silence crackled.

I tried once more. "Seamstress is heading your way."

A collection of sighs filled the earpiece.

"Hun, where are you?" Mom sniffled. "Worried" didn't begin to describe the emotion that plagued her voice.

"I just passed the sushi place that Lightning wanted to check out." Tracking the target's eating habits had more than one benefit.

"Stay there. We're coming to pick you up," Dad asserted.

Soon enough, I crammed myself once again into a van riddled with the stench of sweat. Dad jammed it into gear and sped away, driving right past the church on his way out. Pastor Ben and Katherine stepped along the sidewalk, presumably walking home.

"So, where did you end up?" Tyson asked over the rumbling of the van. "You went completely off my grid."

This was going to be fun.

# CHAPTER FOUR

"I'm fine," I said as I moved down the hall, holding my jacket tightly around its precious cargo. Thankfully, Mom and Tyson seemed far more concerned about my well-being than the way I carried my now balled-up dirty laundry. I turned at my bedroom, catching their concerned gazes. "I just want to be alone," I added.

I closed the door behind me, placing my aching muscles between it and my contraband item. Air flooded my lungs as I pulled the book from its hiding place, making this the first time all day I'd achieved a full, relaxing breath. My fingers traced the faux leather binding. I weighed the book in my hands, slipping my thumb across the smooth edges of its pages.

Eleven hours ago, this book would have meant nothing to me.

Now, I didn't know what to think.

I gingerly pulled the book open, revealing a page full of blank places to print the names and dates of those who had received and given the Bible.

My feet carried me away from the door and I plopped onto the bed, flipping the page. The next section of the book contained a reader's guide, showing me how the Bible was divided and what to read first, depending on what I wanted to learn. Finding the topic of interest, I turned to the section called the Gospel According to John. Despite its appearance in the later pages of the Bible, it opened with, "In the beginning..."

A strong voice penetrated the thin walls. "Sadie!"

I brought my knees to my chest and kept reading.

"Sadie!" This time, the call shook my bedframe.

Sighing, I carefully concealed the book under my pillow and moved toward the source of the noise.

"Yes, Shaw—" I started as I entered his room. Shawn's tired body leaned against his desk, while his eyes searched the gun in his hand for a manufactured flaw. Since I'd ditched my original weapon in Raleigh's lifeless hand, my brother studied a 9 mm handgun identical to the one that made the killing shot only thirteen hours previously.

"What did it sound like when it jammed?" Shawn asked. His broad shoulders seemed to collapse under the pressure of this riddle. Black bags circled his usually bright eyes.

"It just clicked," I answered. "It was like the striker didn't fully engage or the bullet didn't load properly." Shawn concentrated on the gun's barrel, turning it slowly. I continued, "I can't say that I had an opportunity to run diagnostics."

He shook his head. "That doesn't make sense." He placed the weapon back on his desk and brought his hand to his temple. "I checked it before we left. I double-checked it. It shouldn't have…"

"Shawn, it fired the second time. Maybe it was just a fluke," I asserted, touching his arm. "We still finished the job, and I'm fine."

My brother stared at me in a way only a concerned older sibling can. "Fluke or no fluke, I won't let it happen again." He picked the gun back up, moving away from my comfort. "Maybe Dad will have a better idea."

~~

Two days later I was reading the conclusion of the Book of Revelation, ending the section the book labelled as the New Testament.

My door creaked. I dropped my Bible and grasped for a weaponry magazine.

I listened for footsteps and breathing, turning slowly to peek at the door. It remained closed.

I exhaled, waiting just two more moments before placing the Bible back on my lap. But as I flipped back to Matthew's gospel, my stomach groaned a response to the wafting aroma of roast beef. Slipping my Bible under the edge of my mattress, I headed for the dining room.

The alluring smell grew stronger as I descended the stairs and stood in the doorway to the kitchen. Jonathan had the oven open and a thermometer probe in the meat. Mom and Tyson sat at the kitchen island, engrossed in a highly animated discussion.

"Meat's done," Jonathan announced as he slid the roasting pan from the oven. The child-sized apron and floral oven mitts that adorned his broad, masculine frame came into clear view as he pivoted toward the dining area, eliciting a soft chuckle from my lips. Having placed his favourite dish on the table, Jon peered at the island. "Tyson!" he exclaimed, breaking up any possible conversation, "How are the vegetables?"

As if on cue, the pot that had been peacefully boiling on the stovetop erupted with bubbly water. Tyson launched from his seat and flung the pot lid off, stirring the contents. "Done," he replied sheepishly.

"I just hope they aren't mushy," Dean grumbled, finding his spot around the dining room table. "We don't have the spare cash to be ruining food right now, Ty." Mom shot a stern look at her middle son. With the widespread use of the internet, it wasn't a secret that the assassination business had dwindled, taking a large portion of our family's financial stability with it. People would far rather destroy a person's reputation using the convenience of their smartphone than have the liability and expense of ending a life. Although we wouldn't go broke over a pot of mushy veggies, we all knew that the longevity of our livelihood and the secrecy of our existence were ultimately at stake. Some of us (namely, Dean) were a bit more bitter about this fact than others.

That didn't mean we had the liberty to talk about money at the dinner table.

Tyson pulled a strainer from the cupboard. "It doesn't help that Dad's so picky," he muttered defensively.

Shawn stepped into the room. "So picky about vegetables?" he quipped as he walked through the kitchen.

Despite his jovial tone, confusion and concern still stained his forehead.

"No." Tyson lowered his voice. "The Maryland job."

"You know why we didn't take that," Mom stated firmly.

"And it was four months ago. Knock it off," Jonathan added.

Tyson strained the vegetables, speaking through wafting steam. "I'm just saying. I know Maryland is a bit of a…rough spot on Dad's record. But he finished the job, accident or no accident."

"Tyson…" Mom warned. Two footsteps sounded down the hall.

"It's not the accident part that bugs me." Dad's voice boomed through the kitchen as his figure came through the doorway. Tyson froze. I slipped through the awkward pause and sat beside Dean.

"Tyson'll regret that," Dean whispered.

"What bugs me is the person attached to it," Dad continued. "Betrayal is a real problem in our profession, Tyson. If I can avoid geographic areas where I know we've had betrayers retreat, I will. Protecting you is my job. Even though we've silenced them all…" my father scowled, "…there are no guarantees."

Dad finished his brief monologue with a direct stare at each of his children.

I did everything I could not to blink.

The rest of my family all congregated at the table, and the evening meal proceeded as normal. There were no more comments about work, no questions about betrayers, and only one inquiry about why I'd eaten so little.

I blamed the vegetables.

Once we'd finished cleaning up, I retreated to my room. I froze as my eyes found the slight bulge in the mattress where I'd hidden my Bible, unable to pull it out.

"I'm not who I used to be," I whispered. My head fell into my hands while my knees hit the floor.

"Jesus, help me."

~~

"Can I help you?" Tyson asked, not even looking up from his collection of computer monitors. The awkwardness from suppertime still clung to his person.

"Yes, actually," I replied, slipping through the door and closing it behind me. "Can you keep a secret?"

"In this house?" Tyson turned to me and flashed a charming smile. "Only for you, Sadie."

"Okay. So back on that last mission, I met someone," I said.

"Oh, Sadie. You know that's bad news. Remember Uncle—" Tyson moaned.

I punched his shoulder. "I'm kidding." Leaning against his desk, I continued. "I just want to check the footage from the street security cameras."

"I see. And you need me." Tyson stretched in his chair, placing his hands behind his head.

"Only the best." I glanced at his screen. He had re-hacked the security at Raleigh's house. Tyson followed my gaze and quickly closed the window.

"And how is this a secret?" he wondered, probing a little.

"I just don't want the others to know how close I was to being caught. If Mom found out she wouldn't sleep, and Shawn is already a wreck…"

"And if anyone else knew, they'd say something about it. Ironic, for a family with our vocation," Tyson grinned. "Okay, so just cameras? No forbidden love interests?"

"Right."

He leaned into his desk, letting out a sigh. "That would have been more interesting," he quipped.

"Thanks," I said, ruffling my baby brother's already unruly hair. "You're the best!"

"I know." Tyson tapped away at the keyboard, only to stop and say, "Are you gonna gawk over my shoulder the whole time?"

I rolled my eyes and left Tyson's room. Part A of my plan was in order. Next was Part B.

I practically jogged through the hall and headed downstairs to the only other room in our humble dwelling with a computer: Dad's office. Upon creeping through the door, I jiggled the grey power cord out of its place at the back of the desktop unit, rendering the device powerless and consequently useless. Was it a quick fix? Yes, but we all knew that Dad was better with a gun magazine than a computer mouse, so this petty technical problem would be enough for Dad to pull Tyson away from his screen to diagnose the issue.

I'd barely finished my act of sabotage when Tyson called for me.

"Be there in a minute!" I yelled. I whipped into the living room on my way back upstairs. My parents sat on the couch in the middle of the room. Mom's head rested on Dad's shoulder as the radio played soft music in the background.

It was sweet. If only my plan didn't necessitate disturbing them.

"Hey Dad," I started slowly, "Do you know what the weather's like tomorrow?"

"Haven't checked," Dad answered, mildly peeved at my disruption.

"When you do, could you let me know? I'd like to spend some more time outside before winter sets in, so I'm trying to plan my studying around the weather."

Mom smirked at her husband. "She *is* your daughter."

"Sure, Sadie." Dad returned his attention to Mom.

"Thanks!" I pivoted and headed for Tyson's room, having fully completed Part B of my plan.

Purposefully looming over my brother's shoulder, I scanned the screen.

"Look at the church. I know they were still chasing me at that point," I instructed.

Two clicks later, his computer monitor showed the images of five different angles of the church, front and rear.

"There you go," Tyson said as I peered over his shoulder. I checked the time stamp on the image.

"Okay, well, it was later when I ran by," I told him. "But I have no idea how much later."

I watched the recording, waiting for the simple idea of weather updates to nudge Dad into using his computer. Other than being called away to troubleshoot, nothing would separate Tyson from his beloved screens.

Tyson's stomach growled. He stood. "I'm going to find some grub. Want anything?"

Correction: food would separate Tyson from his beloved.

"No thanks," I said. Then I reconsidered. "Actually, what are you getting?" Picking up doubles from the kitchen would take a little longer.

"I don't know."

"Would you make me a sandwich?" I batted my eyes in a sister-like fashion. "Please, Ty?"

Tyson was gone. I had at least two minutes of free reign on his device.

I pulled up a new internet browser window and searched for the local bus station. I had a multitude of dog pictures pop up. I clicked the link closest to the top.

Ninety seconds left.

The page loaded and I entered my departure and arrival locations.

Sixty seconds left.

I memorized the times on the screen. Thursday: none. Friday: 7:30 a.m. and 6:50 p.m. Saturday: 2:20 p.m.

Piece of cake.

I exited the page and resumed watching the security footage. I saw my small body rip across the yard and up the stairway of the church. Only a few seconds passed before I identified the two guards bumping through the street, knocking over the occasional trash can in their path. One pointed to the church door. His partner kept running straight ahead, while he followed me into the church. Soon after, he appeared back outside the door, regained his composure, and sprinted after his buddy.

"Wow. That was tight." Tyson returned with two sandwiches in hand. He handed one to me and changed the subject. "I didn't know what you wanted, so I guessed." A single piece of lettuce accompanied by cheese and tomato hidden between the two bread slices. I glared playfully.

"Grief, thanks."

"You're welcome," Tyson replied with a smile. "You done here?"

"Yeah. Just have to erase the history." I moved the mouse up to the left corner and hit "clear."

"Nice." Tyson's mouth was full of bread. He swallowed. "Would you do it again?"

"Do what?" I kept my tone flat. Would the old Sadie Black be the kill-maker on a mission again? I didn't know.

"Like, directly shoot the target."

"Maybe." I shrugged. "I enjoy being the Seamstress."

Tyson smiled. "Good. I like it better that way." His smile shifted into a frown. "Look, Sadie, I'm sorry about the Raleigh job. I should have known about that other security system."

Yeah, my highly tech-savvy brother should have. The fact that he didn't was a puzzle of its own.

"No worries," I said reassuringly. "All in a day's work." I moved to the door.

"No. Big worries. We could have lost you," Tyson stated.

I turned to face him. Anything I could have said froze on my tongue as my brother's eyes met mine. Left with no other options, I smiled sadly and thought, "You did."

I hurried to write down the bus times that I had memorized and to plan my departure, hoping and praying that the low market demand for assassinations would last another few days. If only for my sake.

# CHAPTER FIVE

Did formulating a plan keep me up most of the night? Yes. Was I confident in the plan I had formulated?

All things considered, not really.

I would leave Saturday at 2:20 p.m., giving me all of twenty-four hours to gather my necessities and depart for a long bus ride.

I flipped open my Bible. To go from reading it 24/7 to not yet today was…different. A not-good kind of different.

I opened to a passage I had underlined: "You therefore, my son, be strong in the grace that is in Christ Jesus…"

A knock disturbed my thoughts.

"Yep," I spoke, hastily shoving the book under my pillow.

"Sadie." Dad opened the door, the hinges crying under the strain of overdue maintenance. "Phone just rang. We have another job." He grinned. "And I want you to lead it."

"What?" I whipped around to face him, social science textbook in hand.

"I'll lead the meeting, but I want you to lead the operation. All of it."

I barely kept my chin from dropping to the floor. "But—"

"We're meeting downstairs, right after supper." Dad left to tell the others.

"Okay," I said to the empty doorway. How could this happen?

I glanced at the clock; 3:04 p.m. flashed on the digital screen. Supper would be served between 5:30 and 6 o'clock.

Two hours was not a lot of time to change a game plan.

I lunged from the bed to my desk, digging through pages of plans from past jobs. I seized the page of departure times and read:

"Friday: 7:30 a.m. and 6:50 p.m. Saturday: 2:20 p.m."

Great.

I snatched my backpack from my closet and stared down the task I'd been low-key avoiding. What would I need to take if I never came back? How could I keep my bag light enough to travel swiftly and inconspicuously?

I glanced back at the pillow. Was it worth what I'd be leaving behind?

I slipped to my dresser, pulling out a few pairs of jeans and a narrow selection of favourite long-sleeve tops and T-shirts. Despite trying to pick out the ones that wouldn't give me away as an outsider, I was left with a surprising amount of black-coloured clothing in my bag.

I weighed the backpack in my hand. I could practically hear Mom say to grab a toothbrush, but my family would notice if one toothbrush was missing from the shelf. My dental hygiene would have to suffer.

I scanned my bookshelf, shooting a quick pang of sadness through my stomach. I wouldn't be able to take any of them. They were not a necessity and would simply weigh me down.

A hairbrush, a notebook, and some pencils entered my bag. I stared at the empty coin purse in my hand. Having never received personal compensation for my work, this coin purse now taunted me with the financial freedom it could have contained (although it had been useful on a job when I was thirteen).

No wonder so few left our family business. No outside connections and no resources equalled little hope.

Regardless, the purse went in the bag. I gazed around the room once more.

"Useless, useless, useless," I muttered. My eyes fell on my grandmother's journal. I reached for it, only to lift my bag instead. It already held a fair amount of weight.

I closed both eyes and breathed.

Grandma's journal had to stay.

My fingers found the Bible under my pillow instead and crammed it into the bag. Pastor Ben's card escaped from the binding and fluttered through the air, landing on the bed. The only two pieces of evidence concerning my Christian conversion lay in front of me. I slipped the card into the bag, only to pull it out again.

If I left it for my family to find, at least they would know why I'd needed to leave.

I set it back on the bed. I stared it down for a few moments.

Scooping it up, I confirmed my decision. If they knew why I'd left, they'd know where to find me.

I wasn't going to be the next name on the Black family's hit list.

With that, the zipper slid along the edges and sealed its cargo. Food was the only other thing on my mind. I had a nine-hour trip before I could hope of being fed again, so naturally food was a prominent concern.

I pushed my backpack under my bed, removing any suspicious items from the direct line of sight.

My fingers grazed the doorframe as I proceeded downstairs. Just once more, Sadie Black would exit her room as the Seamstress. Once more, I would slip into the persona of my old self in order to become my free, new self.

Just. Once. More.

I rolled my shoulders and strode down the stairs, sinking my hands deeply into my hoodie pockets. Unfortunately, my whole family was bustling through the main floor. Tyson followed Dad through the hallway into the training room, cautiously pleading for a new computer system due to the technical hiccups on our last job. Jonathan and Dean wrestled in the living room, perfecting their self-defence techniques. A glance into the open-concept kitchen and dining room area revealed that Shawn and Mom had the dinner table lined edge-to-edge with weapons: pistols, knives, and rifles. They inspected each one for the most minuscule flaw.

On this next job, my family wasn't going to miss the tiniest detail.

"Hey!" Dean called from the living room, "The hermit—" Jonathan's fist stopped the sentence as he slammed Dean's face into the carpet. Dean evaded a second punch and flung Jonathan's body into a couch, allowing him to finish his thought as he grunted, "The hermit returns."

I ducked into the kitchen. "Yeah, hun," Mom coaxed from the table, having heard Dean's obnoxious announcement. "What have you been up to?"

"Just reading," I said as I opened the cupboards. Chips, canned fruit, and granola bars filled the shelves.

I reached for the bars, clutching one in my hand and sliding another two into my hoodie sleeve. I pretended to be searching through the shelves of the pantry.

"Mom," I said, shoving my hands in my big pocket with a huff. The bars dropped from my sleeve into my pocket.

"Yes?" Mom answered.

"Do we have any crackers?" I asked, knowing full well that the boys had finished our last box two nights ago.

"I don't think so. Your aunt hasn't dropped off any groceries lately," my mother responded. As Mom had married into the Black's assassination business, her family still lived relatively normal lives—if you can call high-class thieving a normal profession. They lived in a nearby city, however, and they would pick up and deliver food for a "small" fee. It was a win-win: a little bonus income for them, seclusion for us.

"Okay," I said, pulling out a loaf of bread. I smirked, thinking about yesterday's less-than-desirable lettuce and cheese sandwich. Hopefully, it was the last of its kind.

I finished making a peanut butter sandwich and smuggled a plastic bag into my pocket without further questions. I had nearly made it to the staircase when Tyson turned his attention from Dad to me.

"You nervous, Sadie?" Tyson asked, probably thinking about our last conversation and the "secret" behind it.

"Nope," I said. Technically, I wasn't nervous about the new job at all. Getting out of the house before it happened was a different story.

Tyson smiled. "Good. You shouldn't be with the new tech we're investing in."

"Keep dreaming, boy," Dad declared, confirming that such an upgrade wouldn't be part of this job's budget.

Tyson sighed and Shawn snorted. He hadn't looked up the whole time. His world was shaken; his sense of perfection had been torn.

I was only going to make that worse.

I retreated to the stairs and whipped into my room. I packed the illicit food away and checked the time: 3:30 p.m. If it would take me three hours to walk to the station, as I'd speculated, I had to leave shortly.

Unfortunately, the "leaving" part would be the hardest, both in emotional and physical terms. I knew what our household security setup was, but I'd long had a feeling there were more security measures that I'd never been shown as a kid. My safe haven as a child had instantly become a prison. The four walls that I called my hideout were now four walls of a cell, with only one small window of opportunity.

Thankfully, I could easily fit through that window. I jumped on my chair to remove the flimsy mesh screen. Once that was done, I set to work on the security system surrounding my house, pulling out a small device. Our house, of course, had backup security for its backup security. However, it never ceased to amaze me how one tiny gadget could compromise a whole premise. We had often used this small electromagnetic transmitter to practice or pull pranks in our house. With one click of a button, the electromagnetic waves would jam the electrical pulses in video cameras and sound monitors. It was the simplest way to escape.

I hit the button. The downside of this neat little toy was that it only worked for ten minutes before its battery ran dead.

Time was ticking.

I sprinted to the bathroom to finish my last part of my operation. I twisted the shower's tap and turned the privacy lock before closing the door from the hallway, giving the false impression that I was shampooing, not escaping. Hopefully, this small deception would buy me a half-hour before my family pursued their runaway traitor.

Back in the bedroom, I crammed my backpack through the window, pushing it just beyond my reach. I followed the bag, flinging myself against the wall and scrambling through. Muscular fingers gripped the overgrown grass, ridding my body from the underground abode I'd always called home. I shifted my weight to slide the screen back in place and close the glass pane as far as possible.

"Goodbye," I whispered, pressing a palm gently against the window. I could practically see my younger self, laying belly-down on the bed with her legs kicking the air as she leafed through the plans for her first mission.

Shaking hands hoisted my bag from the ground and strapped it to my back, tearing myself away from the scene.

Six minutes left to vacate the yard.

I bolted.

Now, I've run many times in my life, whether it be from teasing brothers or irate security guards, or even just for training purposes. I've never found running to be a favourite pastime of mine, but as I ran away from my old life, I inhaled the brisk autumn air with a smile on my face. I was free.

It felt amazing.

My steps were quick. My footing was sure. I only had one stop before the bus station—one crucial stop that would make or break my escape.

# CHAPTER SIX

My weary body bounced between impatient passengers as the sounds of the bus station crowded into my ears. I looked at my ticket for the fourteenth time, confirming that I was about to plop down upon the correct seat. My swollen feet tingled pleasantly as my weight shifted off them, signalling a ripple of relief throughout my entire body.

I stretched my neck, forcing my eyes to squint through the window of the bus into the evening sun and peg any potential tails.

Nothing.

I sighed, pushing my hand across my head. Short, spiky locks of hair tickled my palm.

It turned out that selling hair wasn't the easiest way to make a quick buck, nor the most sustainable, but it could be done. The ticket in my hands was proof of that.

I caressed the air where my hair had once been, continuing to stare out the window. Families waited beyond the gate, waving to the passengers that sat all around me. I touched the glass. No one waved at me.

The people I loved the most had no idea I was here.

A sob burned its way up my throat. I pulled my backpack close to me, pressing it into myself as if to stop the bleeding.

I bled anyway.

~~

"Thank you for riding with us." The bus driver's voice buzzed through the speaker system. "Have a great one!"

With that, the pushing and shoving resumed. People jammed their way to the front of the bus, shuffling as if they weren't used to being awake at four in the morning.

Amateurs.

I waited in my seat until they had moved, then proceeded to the door.

The exit of the bus station wasn't hard to find. My small figure sliced through the crowd and out onto the sidewalk. I didn't bother to count how many times I'd checked behind me.

The city looked vastly different than it had during our last job. In the early evening, people hustled around trying to make it home or to the clubs. Now, at the peachy hour of 4 a.m., darkness blanketed the city, leaving bright yellow light bulbs at the end of silver lamp posts to penetrate the night. Buildings, tall and short alike, stood guard over the empty streets, waiting for some thief to steal away their peace.

I stepped past a set of traffic lights, turned right, and found myself walking right past the Raleigh Technologies head office.

In hindsight, a less direct route would have been appropriate.

My eyes fell to the cracks in the sidewalk, bringing my head along with them. Having the Raleigh security guards recognize my face on their cameras would put a serious dent in my plan.

I stopped. If the security guards knew that Nathan Raleigh's death wasn't a suicide, would they have reported it as murder? Or would they keep it quiet due to the other illegal activities Raleigh had been involved with? Was I a wanted suspect?

I leaned down to untie and tie my shoe, hoping that anyone checking the camera monitors would excuse my abrupt stop as a safety precaution.

Standing up, I continued my course as well as my train of thought. In my family's business, as long as the target was dead and we'd left no evidence, the job was complete. I had no idea what happened afterward. Were there police reports? Were other people framed for what we did? What really happened?

With those thoughts fighting for my attention, I kept to the shadows, as far away from the illuminated store windows and glowing street lights as humanly possible.

Once again, my pupils grew big with wonder at how the night changes things. The alleys I'd run into for protection had become shadowy traps for the homeless and the undesired. The sidewalks once pounded upon by busy pedestrians held only the soft echo of my footsteps. I noticed the dead flowers hanging from storefront baskets, killed by the chill of autumn, and the yellow grass still rooted between the concrete slabs of sidewalk.

The softest glow of sunrise warmed the dark sky as the church came into view. Even though they were made of hard, cold stone, stairs had never seemed so welcoming as these leading to my destination. I slumped down on the top step, pulling my knees against my chest and wedging my back between the ornate spindles of the metal handrail.

My sore arms struggled with the zipper on my backpack. I yanked my Bible from the bag, wishing for some caffeine to supplement my dying adrenaline high. Sleep was an option reserved for the weak and careless.

Then again, could a five-minute power nap really hurt?

"Sadie!" I chided myself, shaking my head. I dug through my bag, finding a lone, squished granola bar.

I sighed. Did I have an intricate plan for this stage of my trip? No, but sitting on the steps with a growling stomach and an intense desire to sleep sure wasn't what I'd had in mind.

~~

"Excuse me, are you all right?" a gentle voice broke the haze of unconsciousness. My body jerked awake, whipping my head from its place on my knees and sticking the hair on my arms and legs straight up.

That man was lucky I didn't drop-kick him then and there.

I twisted my face further toward the voice, squinting through very bright sunlight.

He reached for my hand.

"Pastor Ben!" My legs did their best to get up quickly, painfully reminding me of yesterday's events and that my little run wasn't a regular part of my training. I fought to recall how I'd ended up sound asleep at the door of the church.

"Sadie?" Pastor Ben's jaw dropped slightly as recognition struck his features. He seemed as surprised as I was. His darting eyes fixed on where my long hair had once been. "It looks nice," he said, recovering some level of composure.

We were frozen in time for a moment. Ben was no doubt trying to piece together why I was here, sleeping on the church doorstep, looking entirely different than I had less than a week ago. To be honest, I really hadn't processed those facts myself.

"Here, you must be cold," he said, jolting us back to reality. Ben opened the glass door to the church. "Come on in."

I grabbed my bag and moved inside. It wasn't much warmer than outside, but the notion was nice. Pastor Ben went to drop off his belongings in his office. I rubbed at the bags under my eyes, kicking myself for falling asleep. I hadn't even heard the pastor come up the walk. My professionalism had slipped.

Maybe leaving the family trade was a better decision than I thought.

Pastor Ben returned. "Are you hungry, Sadie?" he asked. I nodded.

He led me into the kitchen and opened the fridge. "Help yourself," he gestured. I peeked around the door. The fridge was full of cookies and small triangle sandwiches.

"Thank you," I said, reaching for one of the many plastic containers.

"You're very welcome. Sorry it's not more," the pastor apologized as he poured water into the coffee pot.

"This is great," I mumbled through a mouthful of chicken salad and bread. At the mention of food, my stomach had begun singing a choral piece.

Right now, any food was great food.

Silence held for another moment. Pastor Ben's forehead was slightly contorted, trying to figure out the unexpected events of the morning.

I simply sat at the kitchen island and filled my face with another sandwich. Flavours of ham and cheese danced across my taste buds.

The pastor cleared his throat. "So, why'd you come back?" Ben asked, handing me a cup of steaming coffee.

The sandwich caught in the back of my mouth. How could I explain the last several days?

"It's a long story." I wrapped grateful hands around the warm coffee mug.

"I see," Pastor Ben said, setting his own coffee cup on the counter and pulling up a stool across from me. "Can I help with something?"

He didn't ask about my background. He didn't ask why I was sleeping on the step, or why my hair was gone. Of all the things he could ask, he wanted to help.

Whoa.

"Yes," I began. I recounted the events between leaving the church Sunday afternoon and arriving on the doorstep early Saturday morning, sharing about my inability to be a Christian within my old home. I left out the "assassin" part, and the "I might be wanted by the police in this city" part, but other than that I told him exactly why I was here: I needed to be safe and to pursue my new life.

The hot, bitter coffee consoled my dry mouth and tense nerves as I watched his reaction. His hand stroked his chin pensively.

"Will they find you here?" Pastor Ben queried gently.

"Likely." I tilted my head apologetically. "But America is a big place. If there was someone you knew out of state…"

"I'll see what I can do." The kind man nodded in understanding, placing his hand on the counter. Pastor Ben continued, "Sadie, are you sure that you should be running?"

"What?"

"Maybe you need to confront your family."

A blank stare met his concerned expression. What part of the "running for my life" concept didn't he understand?

Pastor Ben picked up his empty mug and placed it in the sink. "It was just a thought. I'll contact a few people." Ben moved to the kitchen door, analyzing the bags that pulled at my eyes despite my recent caffeine intake. "While I do that, Sadie, I'd suggest you sleep. The sanctuary is empty this morning. No one will disturb you there."

I nodded. "Thanks." With that, we parted ways. Light broke through the windows of the sanctuary, arguing against the pastor's suggestion of sleep. However, my weary body defended his wish as it collapsed onto the row of chairs. My lungs filled slowly, forcing my muscles to relax. Minutes slipped by and I faded in and out of consciousness, avoiding the reality that there were now several individuals wide awake and searching for me. They wouldn't wait for me to be rested to strike.

No one would.

As if on cue, I heard gunfire.

# CHAPTER
# SEVEN

The sanctuary doors burst open. Raleigh's security guards rushed into the room. I dove from my makeshift bed, rolling out of their immediate range and toward the nearest window. A bullet penetrated the glass above my head, sending a spiral of fractures throughout the pane. Hearing footsteps hastily approach my pathetic hiding place, I reached for the chair at the end of another row and flung it at the weakened window, forcing the hole to accommodate the size of a small ex-assassin.

My feet had just left the floor when I noticed shadows in the trees around the outside of the building. My father and eldest brother were poised with scoped rifles. Tyson had a laptop balanced between two branches, and my mother touched her ear. She called the shot.

Next thing I knew, I was falling.

The fall was a rude awakening.

My eyes flung open, taking in my surroundings from my place on the carpet. There were no goons shooting at me, no broken glass, and no family outside. Grief, there weren't even any trees outside.

It had been a dream.

The sanctuary doors creaked. Katherine appeared.

"Hi, Sadie," she greeted me kindly. "I didn't expect you to be awake."

"Or to be on the floor," I thought. I pulled myself back onto a chair and wiped a rogue tear from my cheek.

Katherine sat beside me. "Ben called me. I hear that you won't be staying with us long," she said.

"Yeah." An awkward silence hung throughout the sanctuary. Shaking my head free from my nightmare, I noticed the opportunity that had presented itself. "Do you by chance have a few minutes?"

"Of course." Katherine smiled widely.

I unzipped my backpack, pulled out the Bible, and flipped to where I'd last finished reading. Marking the place was a loose-leaf page filled with questions and concepts that had jumped out to me.

I glanced up to ask Katherine a few questions, but the sparkle in her eye stole any words from my tongue. Excitement and joy filled her other facial features. Her voice emitted a gentle energy when she said, "Let's take a look, shall we?"

With that, I began a two-hour Bible study with Katherine. Her insight, her knowledge, and her understanding spurred more questions. She flipped between sections of the Bible, describing its context and how I could apply it to my life, as well as how all the various parts connected into one unified story.

I lost count of how many times the light bulb in my brain neared exploding.

Eventually, Pastor Ben strode into the sanctuary. When he saw us, particularly his wife, a similar sparkle entered his eye. I recognized this look as pride.

"Sorry to interrupt you, ladies," he started, stepping toward us, "but I contacted Jillian and Adam Baker. They're a missionary couple who have started a church in a very small community in Louisiana, and they are open to having you stay with them, Sadie."

"Perfect," I asserted, allowing a relieved sigh to slip from my lips.

Pastor Ben left quickly. He seemed like a very goal-oriented man. I understood that. I respected that.

"And until you can leave for their house, we'd love for you to stay at our place." Katherine smiled contagiously and chuckled. "Our guest bedroom is a bit more comfortable than these chairs."

I caught her smile and replied, "That would be great."

~~

My mom always swore that the only reason her cooking was so excellent was because of a plethora of stolen recipes—the key word being "stolen." Well, for the first time in my life I was seated at a table covered with food made from homemade recipes, and although the fact that I hadn't eaten much since breakfast the day before could sully my critique, the meal was beyond excellent. So excellent that my mouth was rarely empty.

I had just scooped more creamy potato into my mouth when Pastor Ben piped up, "When would you like to leave, Sadie?"

I swallowed quickly, uttering, "As soon as possible."

"Okay." The pastor looked at his wife, and for a moment they conducted wordless conversation. "We can take you to the Bakers right after the service tomorrow."

My next forkful of food froze en route. "You'll *take* me?"

"If that's all right with you," Katherine said.

"Don't you have to be here?" Surely, they had more important things to tend to than driving across the country.

"I'm sure the intern pastor would be happy to take over my visitation this week," Ben answered. "As for preaching, I can see if the intern pastor or the youth pastor have anything they could share if I'm not back before next Sunday."

"You'd do that?" I could do advanced physics in moments, yet this simple concept of grace eluded me. I could give the Monroes nothing in return. Why rob their time and gas to drive me all the way to Louisiana?

"Yes. We wouldn't have offered, otherwise," Pastor Ben affirmed.

"Thank you." I blinked, processing. The notion was sweet, but the reality of the situation remained: the longer I was with them, the longer they'd be in danger. Their offer was too risky.

"But I need to take the bus. It will be safer for you," I finished.

The couple was quiet. They had no idea whom they'd invited to their dining table.

I found my fork once again and took a bite of savoury chicken, awkwardly awaiting a response.

Pastor Ben ended the suspense. "Okay, we can look into departure times and get you where you need to be."

Katherine still said nothing. She seemed sorry that she couldn't do more, as if my position as a fugitive was her fault.

In some ways, she would have been right.

My plate somehow emptied itself. Pastor Ben found a bus leaving tomorrow evening, and so we planned my departure. Katherine showed me the spare room and left me to sleep.

As I closed my eyes, one number flashed behind my eyelids: 53. Fifty-three hours would have elapsed between my departure from my former home and my departure from this city.

Fifty-three hours; nearly two-and-a-half days. More than enough time for my family to track me down. More than enough time for them to drive here. More than enough time for them to end it all by ending me.

Oh, how I loved my nightmares.

# CHAPTER EIGHT

"See you!" The couple waved from their place on the concrete sidewalk. "God bless!"

I smiled as I weaved to my seat, squinting through the bus windows to see them still standing there.

Before this, I thought that I understood the love and grace of God. Now I saw it in the flesh, watching tenderly and waiting until the vehicle bore me away to safety. If this human compassion was anything like God's, then I had definitely made the right decision in accepting Jesus.

The bus's diesel engine belched, croaking as it heaved us away from the station. I eagerly grabbed my Bible, prepared to make this eighteen-hour bus trip count.

~~

I reached Louisiana with no complications. I made it to the family's farmhouse with no complications. I lived with no complications.

The family was nice. Mr. and Mrs. Baker had two sweet kids, just as Pastor Ben had told me.

I was safe.

Naturally (and somewhat to my dismay), I relaxed. I took myself off guard. I played on the living room floor with the children, wearing any colour but black.

I cracked a joke.

The kids laughed. The simplicity of cause-and-effect worked in my favour. However, in a split second, the cause-and-effect factor flipped backwards on me.

The front door—a few steps away—burst open. Two broad-shouldered, masked men stomped through, both armed.

"Kids, get out!" I yelled, flinging myself at the goons. I knocked the first man's pistol from his grip as his buddy fired several shots. The bullets sliced into the furniture while my momentum carried me to the floor, allowing me to scoop up the first goon's weapon. I turned and repeatedly squeezed the trigger, nearly emptying the magazine before the second man crumpled to the ground.

The first goon froze, obviously mortified by my actions. He then ripped off his mask and howled, "Dean!" I watched my brother Jonathan dive to the fallen man's side, frantically searching for a pulse or some other means to resuscitate our lifeless sibling. Shock paralyzed my body; it had all happened so fast. My hands were drenched in Dean's blood.

Sirens screeched down the farm laneway. Police officers pooled inside the house.

"Hands up!" an officer barked. I dropped the weapon and complied. Cold handcuffs trapped my hands behind my back and an officer's firm grip on my arm propelled me from the house. They were just about to shove me into the cage-like and bulletproof back seat of a patrol car when a final shot pierced the air.

I dropped my focus downward. Blood gushed from my chest. I staggered, grasping the open car door to maintain some level of balance while I scoured the landscape. In the distance, another masked figure drew back his smoking sniper rifle. I didn't have to see a face to know that the shooter was the great Archer.

Dad.

I suppose if my family couldn't take me home, no one would.

I'd be added to the list of Black traitors who'd paid the price.

My body sagged into the officer's arms, which I instantly discovered to be the arms of the bus seat.

I peered frantically out the smudgy window, only to have darkness stare back. I slid my hands up my arms, feeling heaps of goosebumps. Icy sweat trickled down my spine.

"How could I be so stupid?" I muttered, throwing my head back into the headrest. Flicking on the small overhead light, I checked my watch: 3:43 a.m. Two hours and thirty-five minutes until the bus change.

I crashed my heavy skull into shaking hands. I forced air through my nose and out my mouth in a vain attempt to retain a fraction of my composure. Two fat, salty tears splashed onto my lap.

"What am I supposed to do?" I cried weakly to myself.

After a few moments, a simple answer echoed through my mind.

I didn't like that solution.

I dug through my bag, hoping to find the notebook and pencil and come to another conclusion—a better, less "Sadie's-lost-her-mind" one.

My hand gripped the Bible's spine instead. I placed it on my lap, and it fell open to where scraps of loose-leaf paper jutted out from between the pages. Glancing at the highlighted section of Psalm 46, I read under my breath: "God is our refuge and strength, a very present help in trouble."

I shook my head and wiped a few more tears. This only solidified my first, not-ideal conclusion.

My watch reminded me that I didn't have time to argue, even if the argument was a really, really good one. Still, I let a few more seconds tick by before conceding to the inevitable.

"All right, I guess this is what we're doing," I sighed inwardly, peeking upward. "You'd better have a plan for this."

I settled back into the superficial comfort of my seat, desperately waiting for the bus change.

# CHAPTER NINE

Cash wasn't a commodity I was used to. Yes, we needed money to survive, and I knew what a tight budget looked like, but I never worried about actually having or spending it. Perhaps the fact that our family's revenue was gained by extinguishing human life led to my reluctance in handing over those few seemingly irrelevant green bills to the taxi driver as payment. More than likely, it was simply because I'd only been given so much of said green substance by Pastor Ben and Katherine.

"Thanks," the driver said as I slid out of the back seat. I grabbed my bag and slammed the door. The cab pulled away, joining the sea of yellow vehicles that flooded the streets of Washington, D.C.

I stared at the building in front of me, remembering that I wouldn't need money in prison. The J. Edgar Hoover Building—a.k.a. FBI headquarters—resembled a large waffle, and not just because I hadn't eaten lunch. The tan-coloured exterior was indented by many windows and the occasional double-door frame. The structure itself wasn't square, but in some places looked like several buildings had been smashed together. Judging by the crumbling of the exterior walls at certain corners, it would have been a believable story.

I closed my eyes and breathed in. The only story I needed to worry about being believable was my own.

After all, I had to be arrested today.

I stepped past the pillars that stood near the main entrance and pushed the revolving door.

The cameras and sensors were the first things I noticed inside the building. My inner assassin cringed, subconsciously remembering the hours spent avoiding such things. On the other hand, I knew I didn't have any weapons or questionable possessions. Security would be the least of my concerns.

I stated my purpose to the duty guard, who in turn muttered a few words into his walkie-talkie and pushed me through the screening features. It was relatively non-invasive, minus the dog-sniff procedure used to ensure that I hadn't fooled the X-ray machines, but this was no more intrusive than living with four brothers.

Really, security was a breeze.

Another guard loomed on the other end of the screening line and escorted me through several hallways and up a few stairways. The halls were plain; if I didn't know better, I'd have assumed that I'd entered a regular, boring office building.

Once I seemed good and lost, my guide opened a plain door, motioned to a metal chair in the middle of a featureless room, and left.

I didn't need to verify the door was now locked. I didn't need a map to know this cubbyhole room was actually not as far away from the entrance as we'd walked. I didn't need research into human psychology to realize that I'd be sitting for a while, and not because the officers were busy or needed time to pull up my non-existent paperwork. Confinement, disorientation, and time were quite effective at making the average human feel beyond anxious.

I checked my watch. Twenty-one minutes had passed since I'd crawled out of the taxi. Another ten minutes ticked away. I scanned the room, consuming ten more endless seconds. Dull grey walls surrounded me, and I sat on the only piece of furniture. Certainly, there was a camera concealed in one of the corners, and I understood that the deceivingly lifeless mirror in front of me was designed solely to let people hidden on the other side watch me squirm.

I tapped a finger on my lap, meanwhile shaking the leg I'd propped on the opposite thigh. I looked around frequently and twiddled my thumbs. Was I bored? Nope. Did I look bored?

I sure hoped so.

The sooner I looked restless, the sooner they'd end this waiting game.

I checked my watch, this time with the actual intention of reading the time, not just performing for the camera. Forty minutes had breezed on since I'd entered the room. Had I not worn a watch, the constant ticking in the back of my brain would likely have alerted me to this information. Similarly, the stiffness rising from my back notified me of my extensive time spent on this increasingly uncomfortable seat. Was it possible that the FBI invested in research to make such miserable chairs?

More time passed. Finally, the door opened and I heard chatter in the hallway. A young man turned into the room and flashed a smile.

I couldn't help but wonder how accustomed he was to being the centre of attention. He wore his pressed charcoal-grey suit stunningly, and I'd seen smiles like his make other women melt. He definitely wasn't what I'd expected to see stepping through the door, but I'd learned long ago not to bank heavily on mental expectations. Bank on fact.

The fact was that the FBI was smart—at least, enough to think that a young, handsome guy might persuade a college-aged woman to give away her precious information and feel relaxed while doing it. Granted, he could also have been the only operative available, but I couldn't help but doubt that only one person in the entire Federal Bureau of Investigation would have time for a supposed-assassin turn-in. Regardless, I wouldn't be tricked into releasing information.

I would do it purposefully.

The agent pulled a chair in from the hallway and shut the door behind him.

"Sorry I took so long," he said smoothly, as if my waiting nearly an hour hadn't been on purpose. "But I'm here now!" He placed the chair on the floor and dropped casually onto it. "Let's get started, Miss…"

I remained silent. He knew my name.

"…Black," he finished. I nodded and he continued. "Well, I'm Agent Way, and my job is to figure out why you're here. So, what brings you to Washington?" He leaned in and folded his hands, visually investing into whatever I had to say.

I fought back several sarcastic remarks about taxis or politics. "I'm a criminal," I replied flatly.

"Funny," he deliberated. "Normally people run away for that reason." Based on his response, sarcasm would have been appropriate. His tone remained light as he asked, "What type of crime?"

"Murder for hire."

"Ahh…a hitman? Or do you prefer 'assassin?'" Agent Way responded, studying my non-verbal answer to his baited question. You'd think a young FBI agent would understand the power of underestimating one's age, but I had a feeling that the man in front of me thought this was a sorority initiation or something equally dumb. Maybe a research project for the newspaper. A dare made late at night by a drunk student who was too stubborn to back down. I was young. I was a woman. Agent Way wasn't sold that I was an assassin. He was taking things far too carelessly for that.

"Yes," I replied firmly.

"And your name is Sadie Black?"

"Yes."

"Middle name?"

"I don't have one," I answered. Agent Way's questions were coming faster, but his tone hadn't changed.

"Interesting." He reached into his suit jacket and pulled out some folded papers. "Do you have any idea how many 'Sadie Blacks' we have on file? More than one, I can tell you." Agent Way flipped through the pages. "And to boot," he leaned forward and added, "your fingerprints don't match any of them."

This is the part where he was hoping to crack me. The part where I was supposed to be startled that he had my fingerprints although I hadn't consciously given them. The part where I was supposed to make a lame, see-through excuse or outright confess that I'd lied.

I hadn't lied, so no excuse came.

"Humanity is more than papers and fingerprints," I stated. "And there's a reason you won't find mine."

"Such as?" Way raised an eyebrow and grinned.

"I was never given a birth certificate." I tipped my head to the side. "And I've never been caught."

Agent Way leaned even closer and asked, "So where's your proof?" His voice had deepened.

My proof? The graves I had filled over the years, the training I'd received, the fact that I knew more about the gun on his right hip than he did himself. I had plenty of proof but none to show, or so it seemed. Way seemed to pick that up as he eased away.

"You're trying to turn yourself in for crimes that you can't prove you've committed?"

"Well, I could write you a list of names for references." That was the truth.

"Anyone can name a dead man," Way responded, chuckling. This was a joke to him. My fist tightened.

The FBI agent stood and spoke. "You're a girl with no background, no proof, and no motivation to be in Washington, in this chair, right now."

"I have plenty." I stood as well. Two could play this game.

"No, you don't," Way asserted.

"My background comes from the Black family, as you'd know from my name. The Blacks are professional assassins and have been for generations. We've spent years perfecting our craft. I've now left that craft. They'll want to kill me. That leaves me here."

"But why? Why leave?" he pushed, not even fazed by my minor monologue.

"Change in worldview," I said, not skipping a beat. I had a feeling that "Jesus" wouldn't be an answer he'd believe.

Agent Way paused, finally taking in the entirety of what I'd just said. He slipped around his chair, shifting his weight onto the back of it. "Let's say that I did believe you. Capital punishment is still legal in America. Your claim, if verified, would be enough to put you on death row."

I forced back the lump of fear growing in my throat. "I'm sure that would be a judge-and-jury decision, but yes. I understand this."

"Yet you still stand here."

"My family wants to kill me because I have information," I retorted factually.

"The FBI has a lot of information." Way's tone was losing its smoothness, almost as if I'd offended him. He moved to the door.

"Not enough," I argued. He stopped. In a moment, Way's whole demeanor swung from over-confident to slight cowardice. His shoulders slouched and his lungs sighed, ever so slightly.

I continued, "Otherwise you'd know that I am who I say I am."

Way straightened up as he turned to face me, chasing away whatever had plagued him for that split second. He stepped close to me, his bigger frame towering over my vertically-challenged body. He maintained eye contact. "Prove it."

I returned his gaze. Surely, this was all a game. They had to have files on me—at least something on the Black family and our long, lethal history. I'd given plenty of information.

He misread my silence as surrender. "Good day, Miss Black." His harsh jawline revealed a self-satisfied smirk. As he turned back to the door he muttered, "Or whatever your real name is."

Cue Plan B.

I crouched quickly, shifting momentum, and kicked out his knees. As Agent Way toppled, my hand whipped around to snatch the handgun off his hip. I ripped back the slide and aimed.

"Proof," I breathed as the door to the grey room flung open. Several agents burst through, all with firearms pointed at me. I obliged their silent command to drop the weapon and put my hands up.

An agent grabbed my hands and twisted them behind my back. Steel cuffs tightened around my slender wrists.

I had a feeling that I wouldn't wait long to be confronted again.

# CHAPTER
# TEN

New guards hustled me through FBI headquarters. The journey seemed more direct this time, as opposed to my last trip through these halls. I found myself being cuffed to a metal table in another boring interrogation room. The chair was equally uncomfortable.

I guess this was something the good guys and bad guys had in common: poor seating choices.

It wasn't long before I heard gentle footsteps and a swinging door. An older man stepped in. His suit was impeccably pressed, every hair was strategically in place, and his step was quiet in expensive leather shoes. Hard, determined eyes calculated my every move. Those eyes believed they'd seen everything, and their past experiences drove a relentless desire to navigate his circumstances with strength and dignity. Little did those eyes know that I had a similar objective. Older Man closed the door behind him.

"Well, I'd like to be the first to congratulate you," he said silkily as he pulled up a chair opposite mine.

"On?" I asked, somewhat coyly. In reality, I hadn't done anything worthy of congratulating.

"Serving Agent Way's pride to him on a silver platter." Older Man pulled papers from a briefcase beside him. When I didn't respond, he continued, "Everyone needs to be knocked off their high horse once in a while. I was beginning to wonder if I'd have to knock him off myself. You've saved me the trouble."

"Okay." I hesitated to say anything more.

"On the flip side, I have a feeling that's exactly why you're here too. Pride." He looked up from his papers. "I have a couple of questions for you. I assume you'll answer honestly."

I nodded. "Yes, sir."

"Good. Now, all assumptions aside, why are you here?"

"I—"

"Save the 'criminal' stuff. Why are you *really* here?" Older Man interrupted.

I paused, thinking back to the bus trip and the small voice that had insistently nudged me in this direction. "Well, I'm honestly turning myself in for what I've done. That much is true." I spoke slowly but confidently, carefully choosing words. "I'm now wanted by the law and by my family. It just so happens that this…" I nodded to the handcuffs, "is the safer option."

"Shouldn't your family want you?"

"Yes, they should. But not dead." The words flew from my mouth. It was strange how quickly my escape and the consequences thereof had become fact at the expense of my view of a "loving family."

"That's really how they'd want you?" the man pressed, bringing his hand to his chin.

"That's how they've wanted everyone else who's betrayed them," I responded.

"And you betrayed them…how?"

"I'm here. Doesn't that say enough?" I answered, leaning back.

Older Man smirked. "I see." More questions came about my family's line of work, how many generations they'd been in business, and my involvement in that business.

He slid his papers into his case, clasping it closed.

"I wouldn't worry about your safety, Miss Black. Even if you aren't who you say you are, attacking a federal law enforcement officer is more than enough for you to do time behind bars. You'll be staying here a while longer."

Was it appropriate to say thank you?

I opted for a head nod.

Older Man stood and said, "That will be all." He slipped from the room with his case, papers, and my information.

The door clicked shut.

I exhaled. "Thank you, Jesus." My fingers ran along the rough metal edges of the thing I sat on. Maybe miserably hard chairs weren't so bad after all. Death row was still an option, but the hope and peace that filled my heart and mind assured me that this God I followed had a working plan.

Everything would be okay.

I would be okay.

It didn't take long for my escort, Mr. Security Guard, to retrieve me. I had to be the happiest prisoner he'd ever attended to.

He led me into a cell. I imagined that it was temporary. Depending on what they decided to do with me, I'd be moving to a separate facility—one actually designed for criminals.

An amazingly bright fluorescent light greeted me, bouncing its glow off steel-reinforced walls. Only a cot and a toilet/sink unit furnished the small space. I couldn't help but wonder how a real prison would compare. It was something that I hoped I'd soon discover.

Until then, I had plenty of time to contemplate how long "a while longer" would be.

# CHAPTER ELEVEN

7 a.m. — Breakfast delivered.

8 a.m. — Waited for word about my departure.

9 a.m. — Figured out four ways I could break out of the cell using basic cosmetics.

9:30 a.m. — Reminded myself that I needed to be in the cell.

10 a.m. — Mentally balanced the chemical reactions of several lethal substances and wondered if any of them had been added to my breakfast this morning.

10:30 a.m. — Realized this was the first time in years that I had so much free time to concoct absolutely unrealistic scenarios.

10:45 a.m. — Admitted to being stir-crazy.

11 a.m. — Cell door opened.

11:15 a.m. — Stood in an office.

The office was tidy. Wall-mounted file holders kept clutter off the large, oak desk that dominated the space, while shelving with multi-coloured binders broke the monotony of the beige walls. There were no family photographs to be seen, no knick-knacks, no framed certificates boasting accomplishments. The room radiated a distinct sense of blandness; no one could get a read on the person who owned the office based solely on the work environment. Thankfully, it didn't need to introduce me to the person who spent time here. That person had already made my acquaintance.

Older Man motioned me to a chair, simultaneously sending the security guards away.

As I sat, my eye caught the small golden nameplate on his desk. "Bradley E. Richards," its lettering declared. Perhaps the room did have something to offer as a means of introduction.

"You are a very interesting young woman, Miss Black," Richards said while skimming the papers on his desk. My efforts to understand the context of that statement were thwarted because he tilted the documents toward himself. "Much too interesting to be recorded on documents of a low clearance level."

"Thank you?" I assumed it to be a compliment.

Richards looked up. "But definitely interesting enough to be recorded somewhere."

I studied his gaze. "You found proof."

Richards tapped the pages on his desk. "People always have their suspicions." It was as if I hadn't spoken. He continued, "And there have been tips concerning the lives of certain individuals. Threats are investigated; false suspicions revealed. Some are proven accurate."

I waited for more.

"And if the right person digs through those tips, Miss Black, they'll certainly find something. Something that strikes them as odd. Something…"—he paused—"interesting."

"And I fit that category?"

"Definitely. But not necessarily because of those tips." Richards pushed himself up from his chair and stepped to the door. He barely made eye contact as he uttered, "Follow me."

Richards led me into the labyrinth of hallways.

"Do you know where we are?" he asked while looking at me from the corner of one eye.

"Third floor, west side." The words propelled out of my mouth before I registered them. Of course I knew where I was. That's how I'd been trained.

"How long have you been here?"

"Here in this hall or here in this state?" I replied, deliberately qualifying his question.

"This building." We turned sharply to the right, heading down another hallway.

These questions were nothing like what he'd asked me yesterday. "About twenty-two hours," I answered.

"And in this conversation?"

"Five minutes."

He didn't glance at his watch to verify. Instead, there was a command.

"Name something that was on my desk."

"A plaque with a name."

"Whose name?"

"Bradley E. Richards."

He never stopped to say I was right. He didn't have to say anything. "How many exits have we passed in our walk?"

"Eight."

"How many weapons do I have on my person?" Richards quickened his step, preventing me from taking a second look at his "person."

"Minimum one," I immediately replied.

"Minimum?" he questioned, as if I'd answered wrongly.

"I wouldn't assume otherwise."

It wasn't beyond the man to smile. I'd learned that yesterday. Regardless, the way those muscles twitched at the edges of his lips surprised me. From the side profile, that sly grin looked like he had placed a large bet and won.

I wasn't sure whether to feel played or proud.

We slipped around another corner, walking in silence. People strode past us. They barely gave a second glance at the convict in the hall. Did people like me show up regularly? Were all FBI staff so focused on their tasks as not to care? Maybe they were trained not to, or maybe it really did just have to do with security clearance.

Still, Richards and I walked the halls.

We stepped down the emergency escape staircase and along another hallway. Richards stopped and beckoned me to a bulletin board. We'd passed several during our trek, but now he drew special attention to one page that clung to it: the "Most Wanted Fugitives" list.

Richards said nothing; he simply backed away and allowed me to look closer. The list was filled with names and pictures. No one looked familiar to me.

"This, Miss Black, is why you're interesting." His voice dropped to a whisper. "Do you know how many members of your family have been on this list?"

"No."

"None," Richards stated. "But that doesn't mean there shouldn't have been a Black or two on here at some point."

I cocked an eyebrow.

"Your family is extremely good at what they do. I would have concluded the same of you."

"And?" I prodded. Where was he going with all this? Surely this wasn't necessary for a prison sentence.

"That makes you interesting." Richards pivoted from the page and continued walking. I followed. Not only did this building hold a labyrinth of corridors, but also a labyrinth of questions. I had to crack them.

"Miss Black, you have generations of training in that young brain of yours, years of experience comparable to many FBI agents who walk these halls. Now, unexpectedly, you have a conscience driving you to come clean. I can throw all that expertise into prison and keep you locked up for a very long time. Or, I can use it to bring down some other criminals. Make it right." He turned his head to read my response as he finished. "And if I'm not mistaken, that's what you're now interested in. Making it right, that is."

I was at a loss about how to respond. Being behind bars was the only plan I had, yet Richards was suggesting Plan B.

Next thing I knew I was back in his office, and Plan B was being laid out before me.

"Do we have a deal?" Richards reached across the desk for a handshake, revealing his certainty that this offer was one I couldn't—or maybe shouldn't—refuse.

I eyed the paperwork once more. "Just my skills for this job, and then I go free?" I asked semi-skeptically.

Richards nodded.

My mind sorted the information. I knew the stakes. I knew the price. I wondered whether this Plan B was God's plan or an escape plan. I wanted to say no.

Something inside of me screamed yes.

It was the scream that made its way into my right hand, moving it from my side into Richards's firm grasp.

"Yes."

# CHAPTER
# TWELVE

Saying yes and acting on it are two completely different things. Saying it only involves one syllable of three, soft sounds. Acting on it would involve spending the next two weeks researching, studying, communicating, and puzzle solving.

That was a given from the moment I said it. The moment I shook his hand. The moment I had a plan.

What wasn't a given was the way Richards smirked at the establishment of said plan. It was as if he knew something that I didn't—at least, something that I would have cared to know about. That suspicion was confirmed as he lifted a radio unit to his lips and spoke, "Send him in."

Him? Any "him" that we'd talked about in the deal was not within radio sending capacity. He did not have the senator in protective custody, nor any suspects involved in the threat on the senator's life.

I didn't have long to wonder. The door swung open and Richards's grin grew even wider. "Miss Black, meet your partner for this assignment." I turned.

I wasn't sure whether acting on the yes had just become more sweet or more sour. The grimace on the face of the man standing in the doorframe indicated that his vote was for sour.

Richards rose to shake Agent Way's hand. Immediately, Way changed his face from mildly disgusted to dutiful. His pretty-boy demeanor vanished.

"I understand that you are acquainted," Richards quipped rhetorically. We nodded.

"Agent Way," Richards directed, "Take Miss Black to your office and show her the work you've been doing on this project. Time is limited."

"Yes, sir." Agent Way motioned me through the door. I pushed myself up from my seat in compliance, only to look back at the man behind the desk.

"Thank you," I said. Richards nodded and picked up his paperwork as if nothing had happened.

I stepped through the door with Agent Way close behind.

"Left," he spoke curtly, lengthening his stride. He was going to show me there, but only at his speed and convenience. If I couldn't keep up, Way didn't seem to care.

I followed closely down the same halls Richards had taken me through. We advanced quickly down one floor and soon came to an office like Richards's. This one was smaller and had fewer files and shelves, but it was just as uninterestingly tidy. Way unfolded a chair propped against the wall for me to sit on. He curved behind the desk, opened a drawer, and pulled out a manilla folder. The agent flipped through it silently.

My brain switched to work mode. "Where are you at?"

Way handed over a four-page summary of his research. I leaned back in the chair and scanned it: senator's suspicions of a threat on his life, list of potential killers, senator's whereabouts for the last month, senator's schedule for the next two months.

This was what the other side looked like. While I'd been learning how to plan murder, this was how they tried to prevent it.

Weird.

"Pass me a pencil." I reached out my hand. Way rolled his eyes and pushed one across the desk, allowing me to circle the places and times of highest vulnerability. "There are two types of assassin operations," I explained. "Silent and public. Although you can guess how and where they'll be targeted, you need the 'why' in order to pinpoint exactly 'where' and 'how.'" I looked straight at Way and asked, "What's the 'why' here?"

Way flicked through his file and pulled out a more detailed list of the senator's known enemies and their profiles. With each person's name came an occupation, criminal record, family history, and a set of possible motives.

I grinned. Agent Way had done his research. I had the glorious task of seaming it together.

This partnership was turning out to be a sweet one.

~~

"Can I get a background for this?" I asked, underlining key information and flipping the page toward Way. Although my eyes were fixed on my work, my peripheral vision tracked the agent across the desk. He finished what he was reading and glanced at my marked-up page.

"Okay…" He hesitated as he scanned the document, searching for a hole somewhere.

"Agent Way, I just need his background," I said. He reluctantly typed it into the search bar on his computer, then directed the printer to cough up the results in hard-copy form for me.

The faint ink on the page revealed that the printer was just about as tired as I was. I glanced into the paper cup I'd been sipping on since lunch. A few droplets of water taunted me as they clung to the bottom and sides of the vessel, reminding me that Way wasn't about to leave to get me a refill.

To say we had an issue of trust would be an understatement.

Despite this unfortunate fact, my attention couldn't resist returning to the intriguing puzzle before me.

Firm knocking on the office door broke my concentration. A guard poked his head through, announcing that he was there to escort me back to my cell.

I hadn't thought about that in our negotiation of the deal.

"Can you give me a few more minutes?" I mumbled, scrambling to highlight more important facts and references to check. We really hadn't progressed as far as I'd hoped.

The guard stiffened, sending Way a glare of disapproval.

"Okay then…" I directed my focus to a yellow legal notepad, quickly jotting down a to-do list.

"This is what we need to track down tomorrow," I declared, tapping the pencil against the lined paper.

"All right," Way mumbled, still completely engrossed in his own work.

I stood and straightened my workspace. The growing pile of files called me from the wooden desk, pleading for me to stay and keep plowing through them. I hesitated. So many suspects and hypothetical motives stared back at me.

I glanced at the guard. He wouldn't be persuaded.

Sighing, I stepped away from the hours of unfinished work. "Good night, Agent Way."

Way's head bobbed up just long enough to utter a curt, "Night."

Minutes later, I flopped onto the so-called bed in my brightly lit cell, allowing the day's events to settle over me. I wasn't going to prison. I wasn't going to be killed. I would have my name cleared. I would be saving lives for a change.

Can't say that my day had gone how I'd initially hoped.

I was surprisingly relieved by that realization.

My arms stretched above cropped hair, slowly releasing the tension that had crept into my weary body. Heavy eyes opened just enough to notice a backpack, leaning against the grey walls in a corner of the cell. I bolted for the bag, snatched it, and sunk cross-legged into its previous dwelling place. The clothes inside were crumpled after the standard FBI search for weapons or drugs, but the guards had kindly replaced the black Bible on top of all my belongings—just as I'd left it.

A renewed energy and excitement pulsed through my veins as I peeled back the pages to the Book of Psalms and read until my eyelids could no longer keep themselves open. My feet shuffled across the cool floor and tired fingers flicked off the light switch. Upon hitting the stiff cot once again, I fell into the first blissful sleep I'd had in a long, long while.

# CHAPTER
# THIRTEEN

It took a moment for me to remember where I was and what I was doing. I'm sure the sheer lack of sunlight coming through my non-existent window helped with this fact. To think that two weeks ago I'd woken up in my own plushy bed in a pink-walled prison…

Wow.

The moment passed and I prepared for the day. I read my Bible, combed through my hair (during which I realized that I needed to shower), and put on a different shade of black clothing.

The lack of personal hygiene left me wanting, but that would have to be good enough. At least I didn't have a mirror to show me how bad "good enough" really was.

By 8:30, I'd been fetched and was in Way's office, greeted by a bland breakfast on the desk and a cheerless agent behind it.

Way remained hunched over his paperwork. A pile of papers and files sat beside my meal. I picked up a spoon and thumbed through several of the files, noticing that Way had accumulated all the items on my list, from the backgrounds of the most prominent suspects to the minutest details of the senator's schedule.

Impressive.

My dense oatmeal disappeared as I examined the new data in more depth, starting with separating the suspects into piles of "likely" and "not a chance."

"What are you doing?" Way questioned sharply.

"My job?" I returned. "I've sorted the suspects."

"I'll have to check that," Way muttered as he turned to his computer.

I raised my eyebrows in mute rebuttal. Way glanced back at my disgruntled form and leaned in. "Don't expect me to trust your work, Miss Black," he hissed. "The fact that you're only working on this case to save your hide doesn't speak highly of what you'll be doing here. I won't have your lack of care tarnishing my reputation."

"You're only going to bottleneck this process if you keep doing it all yourself," I retorted.

Way grinned. "You're the informant." He picked up my "likely" pile and began riffling through it.

"Oh. I thought the FBI had a lot of information," I regurgitated snidely.

Way paused. He looked at me, recalling that moment in my interrogation. A light of amusement and respect flickered through his eyes, as if strong wit and a backbone held the key to Way's good side.

Wordlessly, he checked my progress and placed the files back on the desk. The corners of his lips fought a smile.

"Looks like we have a direction," he affirmed, marking the beginning of a long day spent tracking down dead-ends and searching for not-yet criminals.

~~

The next day was shaping up as identical to its predecessor. No sunshine, no hygiene, and a guarded transport to Way's office.

The only awkward part about this morning was the fact that Agent Way wasn't there. A bowl of runny oatmeal sat on his desk, and the guard had no problem leaving me alone, so I sat down.

I'd just finished slurping up my tasteless breakfast as Agent Way burst through the door.

"Check this out." Way flopped a file onto the polished surface of his desk. He stood as he typed his password into the computer and rotated the screen toward me. A news article filled the internet page. A vote was coming up in the Senate regarding new laws on monitoring businesses for white-collar theft. Senator Ledger's picture gleamed right beside the headline, suggesting that Ledger had instigated many of the events leading to the vote.

Our shortlist of suspects flashed through my brain and was immediately cut in half. These rumblings of tightening standards for businesses weren't recent news, but the announcement of something happening because of those rumblings could cause many people in illegal businesses to squirm. If Senator Ledger made himself the face of the legislation on top of already having enemies…

The senator had confirmed his own death sentence.

"I assume you've found a similar connection to mine," Agent Way smirked. It seemed he'd fully regained his "pretty-boy means business" attitude.

My eyes darted across the screen as I read further. I could mentally hear the phone call hiring my family to take care of the senator who threatened a business that was thriving, especially if it thrived by unlawful means. I could see the desire for the execution to be public to make an example out of the senator—kill the primary advocate for such a law. After all, if Ledger died of "natural" causes, it might only sway the voting body in Ledger's favour out of subconscious sympathy. If it was a public assassination, a sense of fear or sober reconsideration of such legislation might arise among the members of the Senate. At the bare minimum, one less senator would be alive to vote for such a law. Money would be no object.

I could also hear my father saying no to this job due to its proximity to Maryland.

"Can I see the files?" I asked, scrolling back to the top of the webpage. Way opened the drawer and pulled out our research from the day before. I scanned the list of suspects. We had crossed out many due to a lack of motivation or resources. They could do harm, but assassination was, quite frankly, out of their league. The other half of the suspects fell into an entirely different category.

I flipped to the senator's schedule. If public was the play, the assassin would want a prominent stage. People would have to see it to believe it.

"There," I pointed. Senator Ledger had a ritzy fundraising gala to attend in a couple of weeks. "If something is going to happen, it will be there."

Agent Way balanced his body over the wooden desk and twisted his head to see. "By who?"

"Whom," I corrected. "That, I'm not sure about. Not someone on the list."

Way didn't like that answer. "Meaning?"

I pointed to the remaining suspect list. "Look at them. They all have money. People like them hire people like me to do a job this public. The hitman isn't on the list."

Way tapped his finger on his desk, shuffling through the papers. "So, the senator doesn't attend the gala."

"He has to attend," I replied. "To not show up prolongs the danger and lengthens the opportunity for the job."

"And so your plan…" Way started. It was a question— one that I couldn't just give a concrete answer to. Several plans had already formulated and were bouncing through my mind, but I had yet to knock them down to one.

"We have some work to do," I declared, grabbing the list I'd written the night before. I drew a large "X" through it, flipped the page over, and began jotting down the information that had to be gathered before we could complete the deadly puzzle:

> *Security measures (in terms of both technology and manpower).*
> *List of criminals known as murder-for-hire specialists.*
> *The guest list for the gala.*
> *Direct personal contact details for the senator.*
> *List of resources we had at our disposal.*

"I need this information," I stated.

Way swiped the list and read it over. His prior skepticism shifted into grudging acceptance. "Easy enough. I'll track it down." He reached into his desk, grabbed an access card with a bar code on it, and logged out of his computer before stepping toward the door.

For an instant, Way's appearance changed into that of my brother Tyson—the one who'd gathered much of my information. Had it really been only a week since he'd been saying the same thing to me?

I snapped back to reality. "Hey, Way—" I tried to catch him before he left. The door shut behind him.

Sighing, I glanced around. It had been less than a week, but for some those few days would be an eternity.

I needed a phone.

There was a landline sitting on the desk. I cautiously picked up the receiver and held it to my ear. A dial tone whispered back.

I closed my eyes and visualized the business card that Pastor Ben had given me. I pushed the numbers on the phone, and I waited. The call was completed to long-distance. I couldn't help but wonder if it would be screened somehow.

There was a ringing in my ear. Meanwhile, my head was racing to figure out what to say and what not to say.

Ben's voice came through the line: "Hi, this is Ben."

I started, "Hi Pastor Ben, this is Sa—"

Pastor Ben interrupted. "I'm sorry I can't answer the phone right now, but if you leave your name and number, I'll get back to you as soon as I can. God bless."

The phone beeped and I began my message. "Hi Pastor Ben, this is Sadie calling. I just thought I'd let you know…"

Know what? That I'd been arrested? That I hadn't gone where he'd sent me? "I had a change of plans on the way. I'm perfectly safe, and I'm reading the Bible you gave me. Thank you for everything. Say hi to Katherine for me. I'll see if I can call again sometime. Bye."

I hung up the phone. Hopefully, the vagueness of my message wasn't concerning or annoying. Then again, the whole conversation of "Yes, you housed an assassin who is currently in FBI custody" wasn't a great alternative. So, vagueness. Vagueness would suffice.

The organized desk called for my attention. Way had brought in a new folder, dropped it haphazardly, but had failed to open it. The folder held no "Confidential" classification stamp, so I took the liberty of peeking. The inside held a detailed report of the changes in the legislation concerning white-collar crime. There also was a list of people who'd objected to the changes, both inside and outside the Senate.

Not bad.

I walked to the printer that sat behind Way's desk and slipped a blank page from it. A diploma hung just above the printer. Large cursive lettering spelled "James Anthony Way" above the crest of John Hopkins University, dated only a couple of years ago. Smaller script informed me that Way had successfully completed his Bachelor of Natural Sciences degree.

I cocked my eyebrow. Maybe such a degree was normal for the law-enforcement field?

Maybe there was a story behind it.

I returned to my seat and clicked the ballpoint pen against the desk.

"Who, what, where, when, why, how," I muttered as I wrote those words in a column, then filled in the answers that we currently had. "Who" and "how" were left blank, and I could only partially answer "where" and "when." The only confirmed information we had to work with was "what" and "why": death and crime, respectively.

The door handle clicked behind me.

"That was quick," I said, feeling a slight draft from the opening door. I didn't take my eyes off my list.

"Well, I can only do so much out of this office." Way plopped his findings onto the desk.

I looked up. "What are these?" I asked, nodding to the two cafeteria-style takeout cups of coffee that sat in front of me.

"My best friends when it comes to research." Way pushed one closer to me.

"Okay."

Way tilted his head. "You're welcome."

I ignored the sarcasm and grasped the steaming cup. "What happened to tracking down the information?"

"I have it," he said, reaching into his pocket.

"Where?"

Way tossed prepackaged cream and sugar in my direction. Digging into his other pocket, he pulled out a small flash drive. "Here." He plugged the drive into the computer's USB port and clicked open a file.

"Not all information comes in ink," he said as the computer requested Way's username and password. He entered it, and another window popped up. One hand disappeared into his jacket and resurfaced with the list I'd given him. He handed it back to me and began tapping the keyboard. Soon a list of criminals and their charges appeared, and Way transferred the files to a tablet.

He handed the tablet to me and exited the program, clicking back to his own work. I carefully held the tablet and tried swiping. We hadn't ever had one of these.

Way glanced from his monitor. "Trouble?" he asked, grinning.

I glared. "Could I just have a paper copy?"

Way hit a few keys. "You're killing trees."

I twirled a pen in my hand. "Could be killing other things." Way cocked his head and raised an eyebrow. "But I'm grateful I'm not," I continued. I held out my hand for the printed documents. "We have work to do."

# CHAPTER FOURTEEN

It took days, but I finally held a rough draft of the plan, seeking solutions to the holes within the pages—holes small enough that the public wouldn't see them, but definitely big enough to bury a dead senator in.

I leaned back and propped my feet on Way's desk, reaching my arms far above my head to pull a yawn from within me. My muscles sighed at the stretch, loosening the faint tension of last night's in-cell workout. My hands landed on my scalp, delicately fingering through my freshly washed hair, courtesy of a kind guard who escorted me to an in-house gym for a much-appreciated, hot shower before proceeding to Way's stuffy office. My stomach growled, reminding me that lunchtime was fast approaching.

Way strode into the office. I kicked my feet off the desk and turned to him. "Way, I have a solution for—"

"That's great, Miss Black." Way slipped his coat and scarf from the back of the door. "Do you have a jacket?" he asked.

I raised an eyebrow. "Yes."

He closed the file—my file—on the desk. "Come on."

I didn't try to hide my disgust. "Why?" I asked defiantly.

"You'll see," he responded, opening the door and gesturing me through it. The twinkle in his eyes sparked curiosity in mine, so I complied.

We arrived at my cell, where I quickly donned my jacket.

"Is that all you have?" Way said skeptically from the doorway.

I glanced dramatically around my room. "Unless you see something I don't."

"Okay." Way sighed slightly. He led me through the maze of halls, stopping only once at someone's office, where Way borrowed a warmer coat for me to wear. Finally, we emerged into the foyer. Way flipped his badge at the guard and we pushed our way through to sunlight.

At least, I'd hoped there would be sunlight. Disappointment clung to me like the rainy drizzle that awaited us.

"Did you clear this?" I asked, flipping my hood up.

"No, I'm kidnapping you." Way's slick words slid from his tongue. He rolled his eyes. "Of course I cleared it."

I surveyed the area. How many of the people surrounding us were additional undercover security, not willing to chance a prisoner-turned-informant's escape?

"I assumed that you wouldn't run away, seeing as how you put yourself in your current predicament." Way mistook my glancing around for a desire to locate an escape route.

I increased my stride. "Wrong assumptions happen. I wouldn't hold your breath."

We kept walking. Way pointed out a few of the basic sights of Washington: Department of Justice, Pennsylvania

Avenue National Historic Site, Navy Memorial Plaza. Otherwise, we didn't say much.

After walking around nearly the whole FBI headquarters, he took a hard turn right and reached for a door handle. Way motioned for me to enter, and I stepped into a restaurant. It was more casual than most eateries I'd seen, but it didn't fit the fast-food standard. This place fell somewhere in the middle.

Way ordered food and we found a table toward the back of the room. He dumped a grilled sandwich in front of me and picked up his own, taking a giant bite.

I followed suit. Mayo, beef, and cheese danced across my tongue.

It sure beat a skimpy lettuce-and-cheese sandwich.

I paused mid-chew, remembering the last time I had eaten something this tasty.

Pastor Ben had prayed first.

Swallowing, I put my sandwich on my plate, bowed my head like Pastor Ben had shown me, and prayed silently.

When I brought my head back up, Way stared at me curiously.

I awkwardly met his gaze, but quietly continued with my meal.

Way watched some more, making eye contact between sips of water.

"What?" I asked, dropping my hands firmly atop the table.

"Odd," he said, ripping off a large mouthful of sandwich.

"What?" I prodded.

He gulped. "I said, 'odd.'"

"What's odd?" My exasperation level was steadily rising.

"The act you put on." Way spoke with a matter-of-fact tone. "You don't expect me to believe that you actually prayed just then, do you?"

"I don't expect you to believe anything," I countered, glaring across the table, "But I did, in fact, thank Jesus for the food."

Way merely took another bite.

I crammed more sandwich into my mouth, thinking through our conversation. "Why is that odd?" I uttered, still frustrated by his elusiveness.

Being elusive and cryptic was *my* thing.

The agent picked up his water glass. "People don't just change, Miss Black," Way said, emphasizing my name. "The idea that you held your previous occupation one day and ran away the next because of 'conviction' is unrealistic."

I paused. He had no idea. "Well, Mr. Way, if there's a hole in my act, I'm sure you'll see it." Way snorted. I continued. "If not, then you'll know that people do in fact change, if only by Jesus Christ."

We each chomped at our meals. I interrupted the silence. "Now, what are we doing here?"

"I'm taking you for lunch. Aren't I a nice guy?"

"I gathered that. Yes. What else?" I probed.

"If you must know, we're going to scope out the building where the gala is being held."

"We don't need to. We have blueprints." I had rarely done a job where I'd been in the target area before. Increased visibility led to an increased probability of recognition—and of being caught. Sure, capture was hardly a concern on this side of the law…but the clock on the senator's life ticked on. Our time was far better spent back at the office, researching.

"What if something was missed in the blueprints?" Way questioned. "I want to see it with my own eyes."

I peered at him for a few moments, distinguishing whether this was a difference in training, personality, or intellect.

Soon enough, we arrived at the gala's location: the National Building Museum. Kids with bright-coloured raincoats ran in and out with frantic parents close behind. Some young couples in hoodies held hands as they strolled into the museum, while others just checked their phones despite the drizzle.

The building itself contrasted with the people around it; the structure presented a snapshot from centuries past. Its vibrant red-clay colour distracted from the dark clouds that reigned supreme in the sky, while many long windows teased a glimpse of the elegance that lay within.

That being said, we'd already examined pictures of the "within": the security, the doors, the lighting. We didn't have to be here.

"What's next?" I questioned.

Way cast a superficially confused look at me. "What do you mean, 'what's next?' You're the professional, not me."

"*You* wanted to come here."

"That's right." Way feigned shock. His expression grew serious as he commanded, "Follow me."

We walked into the building. Way flipped his badge a few times to different personnel, and we were soon in the Great Hall, appropriately named, considering its sophisticated balconies, regal arches, and a stunning water fountain. Though it was currently empty, fifteen hundred of Virginia's millionaires, movers, and shakers would gather in this historic place one week from today.

As jaw-droppingly beautiful as this heritage architecture was, nothing in this room was new to me; the construction of the walls and pillars reaching to the high ceiling had all been studied. The intricacy of the flooring and drapes had been analyzed. Grief, I probably knew the air ventilation system better than the top security guards who worked here. I didn't understand why we were wasting precious time.

Any information we needed, we had.

"Are you done?" I whispered as politely as possible to the figure in front of me.

He turned. "Is there truly nothing you would want to test here?"

I brought my finger to my chin and tapped it. Within a few seconds I jumped. An exceedingly small echo followed the sound of perfectly worn-in sneakers hitting the floor. That wouldn't be heard through the chatter of a party.

"Hey!" I yelled. A larger echo followed. Way didn't have to fake his shocked response; this time it was very real. Smiling and shrugging at him, I simply explained, "Acoustics." I repeated the exercise with a few different tones and pitches. Even when this room was fully occupied, it would echo. If a gun was fired, the world would hear it.

Then again, if a gun fired, we'd have already lost.

How stupid.

"I'm done," I concluded.

Way walked around the huge room some more. He appeared to be mentally charting where everything would be placed on gala night.

He came back to the doorframe I was leaning against.

I straightened. "Contented?"

"Very," he answered, striding past me. His shoulders cemented in self-satisfaction as we returned outside. Something had flicked on in his FBI brain.

Meanwhile, I cringed. The clouds had parted, leaving my once-coveted sun to act as a spotlight on the two of us. Thankfully, no one paid attention as we walked down the steps and onto the sidewalk—no one except two men on the opposite side of the street. One read a pamphlet as he strolled by, glancing up occasionally in our direction. The other manoeuvred a camera on a tripod, taking pictures of the building while effectively capturing the image of the ex-assassin who had just exited it.

I quickened my step.

Fighting the urge to look back at these two gentlemen, I wanted to discount the uneasiness I'd gained by their presence. However, these feelings coincided with a fact I knew well: unnecessary exposure meant unnecessary complications.

I couldn't shake the feeling that I had just acquired both.

# CHAPTER FIFTEEN

"Here we go." Way adjusted his gold cufflinks. He winked at me through the mirror as he centred his tie. I rolled my eyes and tugged a ripped baseball cap over my short hair.

Way, being the natural actor he was, dressed the part of a young heir with a desire to meet beautiful women at the gala (which I imagined was a fairly accurate addition to his motivation to watch for anything out of place). I was his perfect contrast. I sported a look of homelessness and a stench of filth (which, again, was fairly accurate since I had no home or shower apparatus to call my own). Way and other well-dressed agents would attend the prestigious gathering, while a handful of us disguised in dirt and rags would monitor the scene from the outside.

Not a bad gig for the informant.

"Don't break too many hearts, okay?" I teased as we headed for our vehicles.

Way shrugged. "I'll try. Don't attract too many scavenging cats."

I laughed as I slipped into the black SUV. "I make no promises." The door slammed, trapping four agents and me in the two back seats.

My head fell into my hands, and I blinked back fatigue and restlessness.

That last outing had not been good for my psyche.

The driver dropped us off in a gloomy alley two blocks from the National Building Museum. We dispersed and located our posts.

"Black, you in position? Over," Richards questioned through the comms network. He was orchestrating the finer points of the operation from the comfort of FBI headquarters.

"Yes. Over." I leaned against "my" tree, hearing a symphony of fallen leaves crunch underfoot.

Sliding into a relatively comfortable, seated position, I shook out my arms in an attempt to ease my anxiety. "The LORD is my shepherd…" I recited under my breath, watching guests funnel out of expensive cars onto the sidewalk. Couples sashayed into the brick building, dressed up beyond practicality. Stiletto heels and snug cummerbunds would be of no use in the event of a crisis (unless, of course, the cummerbund was to be used as a weapon, which had proven effective in my personal experience). Universally, groans and complaints about the heavy security wafted from the arched entrance to my humble tree.

They had no idea.

Within an hour, the front doors closed and the gala officially began, leaving me to watch the stationary doors of the National Building Museum for another four hours.

Lovely.

"How is it, Bluebird? Over," I queried Way over comms. Different organization, same concept.

"It is a fine evening," he responded, "but the punch is a bit bland." Code meaning: "It's going well. No sign of anything." If the punch became lively, he had a target.

"Outside patrol, report," Richards commanded. We had the same message: no sign of anything.

We waited. I checked the time. It was 6:14. The senator would be giving his speech at 7:30.

6:30 p.m. — Nothing.

6:45 p.m. — I wanted some of that punch, bland or not.

6:50 p.m. — A young couple snuck outside to make out. I reported this.

6:55 p.m. — I would have thrown up the punch, courtesy of the two lovebirds.

7 p.m. — Couple went inside.

7:01 p.m. — I started to inform Richards that they'd left.

Nothing but buzzing met my ear.

"Does anyone copy?" I hissed.

"Buzzzzz" was the only response.

Movement rustled the dead leaves near the trees across from me. Shadows of two individuals raced to the corner of the building opposite mine.

Before I could object, my legs carried me toward the shadows. The agent who was supposed to be on that side of the building clearly wasn't there, and it wasn't like I could tell them anyway.

Both shadows crouched tightly against the National Building Museum, waiting.

Shadow One glanced through a window. He must have motioned to the counterpart, because Shadow Two took out a device and tapped the old glass. It broke in a few places, making a large hole. Both shadows slipped through it.

I waited for an alarm to go off. Nothing happened. Buzzing still filled my ear.

I glanced toward my tree, then back to the broken window. Adrenaline and urgency forced my decision. I rolled to the wall, pinning myself against it before entering.

The sound of the breeze picked up slightly. I glanced up to see a body slide from a neighbouring building to the roof of the National Building Museum by a sleek, zipline-like contraption.

My head rested against the brick wall while I breathed, "Jesus, help me." I pulled myself onto the ledge and leapt between the shards of glass, landing noiselessly on the hardwood floor.

A slight mud trail revealed the intruders' route. I ran the other direction, dodging the individuals who would doubt my intentions and praying that the two who broke in would get lost. It was unlikely, but it was my prayer, nonetheless.

I hit the stairs and whipped myself up toward the ballroom's first balcony. The gala room was dimly lit, while the renowned musicians did an excellent job of filling the Grand Hall with live music (an impressive feat due to the sheer size of the place). The cocktail chatter kept up to the volume. Servers slid effortlessly through the spaces amid the crowd, offering several mouth-watering varieties of finger food.

It was a perfect setup for murder.

"Where are you?" I muttered. Finally, my eye caught sight of Way, standing five paces from Senator Ledger. I scanned for my unwelcome friends from outside, both high and low.

When that failed, I routed the quickest path to the senator. I flipped over the edge of the balcony and landed softly on my feet.

I sliced through the crowd. As I passed Way, I simply grabbed his arm, tearing him from his pleasurable company.

"Breach," I snapped, tapping the comms unit in my ear. I pulled him to Ledger.

"Mr. Senator," I addressed him quietly from the side. As he turned in my direction he gaped at my dirt, as if my dirt would hurt him. I continued calmly. "There has been a breach. I need you to come with me."

The senator looked at Way for an explanation. I stared at Way, willing him to validate my statement.

His face disappeared, along with the faces of everyone else at the gala. The world flung itself into a dark unknown, along with the likelihood of the senator's survival.

# CHAPTER SIXTEEN

The room's noise level fell to a whisper. "What happened to the lights?" popped through the hushed tones from a plethora of voices.

Unlike the affluent guests, my concern wasn't that the lights had gone off. It was that they hadn't flipped back on. Way and I had set up two precautions against this: backup power connected to the lighting, and security people stationed by the breakers.

Something should have happened by now.

Three other elegantly dressed agents now surrounded the senator and moved quickly to escort him out.

The lights finally flickered back to life, and with them came a familiar voice over the comms unit.

"We are back on. Over," confirmed Richards.

The crowd slowly picked up their previous conversations. The lights were nothing but an inconvenience to them. It was an old building, after all.

If only they knew.

Way moved closer to me. He leaned to my ear and whispered, "You might want to leave before your appearance draws unwanted attention."

"That's a minor concern right now," I hissed. I kept one eye on Senator Ledger. The agents maintained a looser circle around him than they had a few moments prior, but they still hovered within his reach.

Richards's voice came over comms. "Black, move. Over."

"Ten-four. Over," I responded. "Watch him," I advised Way firmly as I strode toward the exit.

Call it intuition or years of knowing better, but I wasn't going back to my tree. Not over the senator's dead body.

Instead, I headed for the balconies. Yes, there were cameras up there, but I couldn't say I was confident in our resources at this point.

My grimy but agile frame ascended the stairs, passing both the first and second levels. The sounds of the gala resounded off the ornate ceiling as I stepped onto the third balcony.

"Black, where are you?" Richards growled, "You're supposed to be—"

"Top balcony. Over." I interrupted, pivoting to the nearest security camera and giving a small wave.

"No visual. Over," the veteran agent responded.

Urges of fear and curiosity slashed my stomach. Turning my face from the camera, I whispered, "Our eyes are blind. Over." The reality was that our eyes were worse than blind. They were deceived.

My mind played out the scheme. Someone had hacked into the cameras for the entire building. Meanwhile, we were left with looped tracks of empty halls, despite the extra encoding we'd put in place.

The enemy knew more about my location than my allies. That was never a strong position.

The comms crackled, "Find out what they are hiding. Over." Richards sounded equally reluctant and supportive.

"Send the indispensable one," I muttered, looking for anything that could serve as a weapon. I wasn't allowed to be armed, and I couldn't say that I wanted to go into potentially hostile territory without protection. Unfortunately, that was my only option.

Great.

My steps stayed light. No sound escaped my lips, and my eyes examined every crevice and shadow. My brain poised itself to be ready for whatever was at the end of the hall, although part of me hoped I'd never find out.

The sight of a man cut my walk short. Seeing his face, my breath caught in my throat.

"Excuse me," the man said, "But I don't believe you're allowed up here—"

My head stayed bent. "Sorry," I mumbled, throwing my voice deeper than normal. I turned, snatching a glance at the rest of the balcony. A shadow shifted behind one of the stone arches. A narrow barrel poked from around the corner.

My step quickened, travelling out of an earshot.

"Suspect has been spotted and is armed, over," I stated, not breaking stride. At least now I knew where the threat was.

I also knew we were up against the best.

Richards quickly replied, "Were you seen? Over."

"Yes."

The line was quiet. Richards, the man with all the answers, fell silent.

Another agent piped up. "Should we move the target? Over."

"Not yet. Keep close tabs," Richards asserted. "Bluebird, meet up with Black and confirm the suspect. Over."

"Black, janitor's closet. Over," Way commanded.

I checked my watch. In fifteen minutes, Senator Ledger would be giving his speech.

"No time," I responded. "First balcony."

Way met me shortly. He pulled his comms unit out from his ear.

"Where is he?" Way asked.

"*They*," I emphasized, "are up there." I tilted my head. "I'm sure they have eyes everywhere."

"Do they have ears?"

"Unlikely," I said. The Black family rarely used those techniques. "But I'm not risking that one."

Way scanned the area. A plan bloomed in my mind's eye.

"Grab my arm," I said.

"Why?"

My eyes widened and my tone was obvious. "I'm not supposed to be here."

Step one of plan: get me away from the balcony. Their target might be the senator, but they wouldn't withhold a second shot.

He grabbed my arm. I struggled. He held on, confirming that he understood what had to happen.

He pulled me close. "How many are here?"

"Six. At least two are on the third balcony," I whispered, still twisting in his grip.

"Great." Way shoved me along, leading me off the balcony and through the door. "We'll take it from here."

Keeping my head down, I exited. Way headed back to the balcony.

I was effectively out of the picture, unaffiliated with anyone else. I could go outside and wait by my tree—unseen, unheard, and unsuspected.

I headed back to the shards of the broken window, piecing together the plan that my family must have concocted. My family used the building beside this one to reach the rooftops. Tyson was monitoring from a van, and at the right moment, he turned off the security systems. Dean and Jonathan would be watching Dad and Shawn to prevent anyone from getting too close (like me). Mom could be anywhere, although I imagined she'd also have come in through the roof.

A guard stood by the window now, no doubt having called it in. I put both hands in the air. "I was just leaving," I said, eyeing the broken glass. This was one piece that didn't click for me. Why would my brothers break in via the window, where others could see, if they could just use the roof?

It went against everything we'd ever learned or trained for.

"Shoot," I groaned, mentally kicking myself. I wasn't off the hook yet.

"What?" the guard said, creasing her forehead and slipping her hand to her gun belt.

I glanced at my watch. Ten minutes until the speech.

I made eye contact with the guard and touched my ear. "There is a second breach," I relayed into the comms unit. "Get the senator out of there."

No immediate response. "Do you copy?"

"Where?" Richards questioned.

The painful reality hit. "I don't know," was all I could say.

Two loud pops pierced the air. Shrill screaming followed.

My legs ran back to the Grand Hall before I realized what I was doing. I passed two agents carrying the senator, heading for the safe place. Based on the red liquid gushing from his chest, they were too late.

Another agent hobbled out of the ballroom into the hallway, clutching her side. Blood oozed through her fingertips. A fellow operative quickly wrapped his arm around her waist to drag her away from further harm.

I froze.

The earpiece filled with commands. Richards shut down the exits. Way assured us that his suspect hadn't fired. His partner reported that the intruders had disappeared before they'd reached the balcony. Another agent was tracking where the shots had come from.

In the din of the gunfire's aftermath, no one else noticed the man zipping out of the ballroom and down the hall toward me.

"That's one," I muttered. I quickly crouched to intercept the once-shadowy figure, but a second individual stole my attention through the open doors of the ballroom. A light of familiarity flickered deviously across his face, causing him to raise his sleeve to his mouth. I urged myself to run.

I wasn't fast enough.

Another shot rang out from down the hall. I no longer saw the running shadow-man, but I felt his legacy. A bullet grazed my left arm before penetrating the wall behind me.

The other man sneered. I sprinted out of his sight to the front entrance, snatching a gun from a preoccupied security guard. I busted through the main doors to see the hitman from the hall slinking along the darkened street.

"East side!" I yelled, but the comms line was too busy for the others to hear.

The gun in my hand released several shots, purposefully catching the hitman's feet as he broke into a dash.

Another agent started a pursuit upon hearing the shots. I lowered my weapon.

I rushed back to the ballroom, returning the grabbed handgun en route. I scanned for the other man. He was gone.

My mental clock ticked. My family would also be gone.

A sea of adrenaline filled the ballroom. Frantic guests elbowed their way toward the exits, not realizing the threat had already disappeared. Security staff moved quickly to block the doors, but the panic-stricken people shoved forward, creating a human current that would not be stopped by mere man.

Women tripped over heels and skirts. Men who stood a head above the others scanned the premises. They all rushed for safety.

I studied the crowd, hoping for one last glimpse of the running shadow's cohort.

I saw her. She wasn't the shadow's ally by any stretch, but as those eyes cut into mine, recognition dawned in them. Her red lips parted as her jaw dropped, allowing the name "Sadie" to escape. Although my brothers had missed me, my mother identified me in a moment's glance. The tide of moving people immediately swept her black gown and dark hair away.

The comms unit still clamoured with nonstop commands. A burning sensation crept through my arm, but diverting my attention from the guests wasn't an option.

The ballroom had been effectively drained when Way and his fellow agent descended from the balcony.

Way nodded at the other operative, who proceeded through the door. Way stopped at me.

"They were gone?" I questioned softly.

He nodded. "We had just reached the balcony when the shots were fired. Never saw them. Did they have backup?"

I shook my head. "They had a rival," I told him. "And the rival took the first shot." They'd also taken the second and the third. I raised my right hand to the place where the bullet grazed. My hand was met with a sodden sleeve, drenched in blood.

Maybe it'd been a better shot than I'd thought.

Way glanced at my wounded arm. "Are they still here?"

"Blacks or the rival?" The cut was bigger than anticipated.

"The rival," Way clarified, surprised at my reference to my family.

"I don't believe so. He disappeared when the crowd did." I said absentmindedly. There was a lot of blood.

Way opened his mouth to speak, but Richards's voice came through. "Bluebird, do you copy?"

"Yes sir. Over." Way held up an index finger, instructing me to give him a minute.

"Ensure everyone has exited the building."

"Yes sir. Over," Way confirmed.

"Black, get yourself cleaned up," Richards ordered. "We already have one mess to deal with."

"Yes sir." I entered the bathroom, cradling my wounded upper arm. The burning intensified as I scooped lukewarm water from the tap over it. The filth from my costume had already infected the wound, evident by the blood and dirt that washed out. I moistened a thick wad of paper towel and pressed it to my arm to attempt clotting.

I studied the girl in the mirror. My hat and tattered clothes clung to my sweat-covered skin. Blood had managed to splatter onto my pants, and my hand over the paper towel attested to the proximity of that bullet hitting my heart. Had it been another hand-width over, I wouldn't be standing in the bathroom.

I shuddered. Death had almost ended me, proving my nightmares to be more than just dreams.

Death could still end me. It was just a matter of strategy.

# CHAPTER SEVENTEEN

My cell held bittersweet feelings: sweet in the manner of providing safety, and bitter in the manner of holding the failures of the night before.

I didn't know whether or not the senator made it. I didn't know what they'd found. In fact, the FBI team did an excellent job of keeping me—the direct blood relative of the attempted murderers—completely uninformed.

I lay on my back and stared at the ceiling, replaying the evening in my mind and waiting for it to be over.

My right hand slid up my opposite arm to touch the wound. It was now treated and bandaged, and the burning had subsided. The fear associated with the burning, however, lingered.

My Bible sat open beside me. I had already flipped to several passages in vain attempts to distract from the dreadful evening. I shifted to my side to read them all again. "He will wipe every tear from their eyes. There will be no more death or mourning or crying or pain, for—"

The door opened behind me. "Black?" I turned. Way stood in the doorway. "They want you."

Way led me directly through the halls. There were no unnecessary turns, no speed changes, no clever gags to throw off my sense of direction.

We entered Richards's office. The older agent bent aggressively over the desk while another, unknown man froze mid-step beside it. By the looks on their faces, the discussion they'd just ended had been a heated one.

About me.

Richards gestured to a chair. I sat. Way hung back at the door, giving the men as much space as possible to sort out what exactly had transpired at the gala.

"Miss Black," Richards started, keeping a cool tone, "How many threats did you say there were?"

"Two. The unknown assassins and the Black team," I responded. I could tell the other man was not sold on my answer.

"Yes. And you reported both of these promptly?" Richards probed.

"I did."

Richards's expression was smug as he focused back on his colleague. "Anything else?"

The taller agent glared down at Richards through cold, grey eyes. A lean man in his late forties, his hair was sprinkled with silver streaks and his face was stone-set.

"What happened this evening?" the agent asked me. It wasn't a brilliantly framed question, but it hit the mark.

"The senator was shot," I responded.

"Yes. Before that," he clarified harshly. I relayed the facts of the evening—how I saw them break in, when I encountered both parties, when I tried leaving.

Richards grinned slyly as I spoke, clearly satisfied with my account.

I ended my narrative by describing how I'd run back to see what had happened. The man seemed less than impressed, as if I'd neglected an important piece of information.

This disgruntled agent turned his attention to Richards. "I still hold my view."

"This evening is about facts, Martin. Not views," Richards returned. A brief silence followed. Richards broke it with, "Was there anything else?"

"No," Martin said, flicking his wrist. "Not until you think logically about the situation." Way moved from the door to my chair. It was time for me to leave.

"Is the senator okay?" I asked, still seated.

Martin studied my face while Richards replied softly. "He's recovering. The shot wasn't accurate enough to be fatal."

"I figured it wouldn't be," I said, subconsciously touching my bandaged wound. After a moment, I hastily dropped my hand to my lap, lacing my fingers together and pushing that thought from my brain.

It was still too real.

Martin once again turned to Richards. He didn't say a word, but I picked up the purpose of such an interrogation and the sparring agents' non-verbal communication.

"I wasn't a part of it," I stated. "I prevented his murder. I didn't instigate it."

"I never said anything of the sort," Martin declared defensively.

"Yeah, you didn't have to," I returned.

The agent looked at Richards as if trying to prove something. Richards spoke. "She's done a lot of things, but not this one."

Martin opened his mouth only to shut it again. He breathed deeply and stepped back. "Richards, it's your case." His tone was more similar to Pontius Pilate's "I wash my hands of this" action than to giving in. Martin was prepared to watch Richards crash and burn.

"And I'd appreciate you treating it that way," Richards replied evenly. He moved back and sat in his chair. "Thank you for your time, Agent Martin."

Agent Martin nodded and turned to the door. Way stepped promptly out of his path, and Martin left without another word.

Richards exhaled sharply and tapped a few strokes on his keyboard. The printer sprung to life behind him, spitting out several pages. "With that out of the way, we can move on to more pressing matters." Richards spun his chair around to the printer, snatched the sheets and placed them in front of me.

"What are these?" I asked. Way came closer to see for himself, while I remained stationary.

"One is the statement that you need to fill out as a witness present at the gala," Richards said. "And one is your expert theory on how it happened from an operative's perspective." I gingerly grasped the paperwork. A clean, crisp format ensured the documents had plenty of large empty spaces to hold my answers.

"I expect your report first thing tomorrow. It's best to write it fresh. Don't sleep on it." Richards dismissed us.

At the cell, I studied the papers in my hand. I sat down on my bed, using my Bible as a temporary desk, and wrote out my witness report. After checking it for proper grammar and sentence structure, I worked on my hypothesis of how those same events played into the attempted assassination. The lone incident that seemed random in the whole scheme was when the lights went out, only to come back on within forty-five seconds without using either of the preventions that Way and I had set up. I speculated that one of the attempted parties (most likely the unknown assassins) had shut down the lights to sneak into the ballroom and kill Ledger. The Blacks, realizing that the sudden darkness would look suspicious, reactivated the lights ASAP to preserve their cover.

Realistically, my family's plan of using the cameras against us, sneaking in from the roof, and having hit team members dressed like guests and security guards would have worked extremely well to assassinate Senator Ledger. I imagined they would still have had ample opportunity to take the shot during the speech. However, the unknown assassins completely sabotaged those efforts as they literally countered every element of the Black team's plan, from breaking in through a window to opening fire when the senator began to leave.

Ironic.

Placing my completed paperwork on the floor, I rolled into a horizontal position on the hard cot, officially ending my evening.

~~

I was dreaming. I knew that. I knew I was sleeping. I knew I was safely tucked away in the J. Edgar Hoover Building.

Somehow, however, I lived back at the gala. The party itself became outrageous. Clearly, the punch was no longer bland but spiked with some form of strong alcohol. The music blared. The guests yelled. I was in the middle of it all, but this time I was dressed like the rest of them. A long, royal blue dress cascaded from my shoulders, causing my sapphire eyes to sparkle. My feet were trapped in those pinchy heels that prohibited movement.

I saw my mother. She held a glass between gloved fingers as she flirted with one of the other senators. A large space opened between her and the crowd directly behind her, but she didn't notice.

She also didn't notice the gun that a man had trained on her back.

"Mom!!!" I tried screaming, but my voice blended into the deafening sounds of the party. My heels were glued to the floor, and my hands were pinned to my sides.

The gunshot exploded and my mother sank gently to the floor, her cocktail splashing across the intricately patterned tile. My brothers and father charged to her aid, but five more shots burst through the air. I tried to look away, but I couldn't. One by one, each man dropped to join my mother's body. No one else paid the slightest notice. No one else cared about the trickling blood that pooled around their lifeless bodies.

I cared.

I did nothing.

# CHAPTER EIGHTEEN

"Here they are," Way said, putting our combined paperwork on Richards's desk. He barely gave it a second glance.

Way's demeanor was solemn as he motioned for us to leave. I stepped forward instead.

"Agent Richards," I asserted, "Is there any paperwork that I need to fill out for my release?" With my family now clearly aware of my association with the FBI, this building was the last place I wanted to be. Somewhere far away and under witness protection was definitely the preferred option.

Richards remained hunched over his work. "Not today, Miss Black."

I cocked an eyebrow and pressed the issue. "Tomorrow then, sir?"

Richards put his pencil down and made eye contact. "Due to current circumstance, we can't afford to let you go at this point. You'll continue to work with Way until we catch the criminals responsible for last night's events."

I glanced at Way. His weight shifted uncomfortably from one foot to another.

"What about the deal?" I directed my attention back to Richards.

Richards breathed deeply. "The deal is still valid. It's just on a temporary…" he fought to choose the appropriate word, "…sabbatical."

I drew my breath to retort. All that came out was a highly tensioned, "Yes sir."

Way and I left the office. The halls felt narrower than they had earlier. The ceiling seemed closer to my head. The reality that there were few windows to jump from made this place that much more claustrophobic. Way's office was no better.

We sat in our respective spots. I kept my posture straight, my breathing slow, and my tone even. "What do we have to do today?"

Way's concerned, brown eyes watched me. I stared down at my black-and-white sneakers as he read my body language, obviously recalling the events of moments before. The look of weariness he'd worn all morning dissipated through explosive laughter. "At least I know my partner isn't a robot," Way squeezed out between breaths.

I crossed my arms. "Excuse me?"

Way coughed and brought his outburst under rein. "With as little emotion as you show on a regular basis, I was concerned you weren't actually human." His tone began on the light side, ending as cautiously playful—both regarding his uncertainty about the night before and my present emotional state.

"Doesn't this bug you at all?" I snapped at him. In my mind, I began a monologue about how we'd made a deal that if I helped prevent Senator Ledger's death (as I had) it would be arranged for me to leave clean.

"Oh yes. But I can't change Richards's mind. If I could have, quite frankly, you wouldn't have been here—" Way gestured to the very familiar office, "—to begin with. But you're probably the only reason that the senator is alive today, so you get to sit your butt in that chair and work with me until we see our suspects behind bars."

I froze.

Way was right.

And that was terrifying.

"Fine. Where do we start?" I complied reluctantly, my mind far away from the issue at hand. After all, if I kept Senator Ledger alive, who would save me?

~~

No matter how hard I tried to move on, Way's statement and my question hung over me like hefty storm clouds. It was fairly easy to ignore them while working in the office or bickering with the cocky agent behind the desk, but the moment the cell door clicked shut, I was alone with the gruelling thoughts of an anxious mind. Oh, what I would have done to have one of my brothers burst into the cell and crack a lame joke to make me smile, or for Mom to lovingly interrogate me until I finally stopped hiding my fears and emotions and confided in her. Pastor Ben, Katherine, or even the Baker family in Louisiana would have made wonderful company, especially when compared to the faint echo of my own desperate voice against the cold, sterile walls.

I left my Bible open on the cot so encouragement and distraction were only ever a glance away.

So, I prayed.

And I read.

And I reminded myself again and again that Jesus had already saved me, that my life was in His hands, that He had successfully brought me this far, that I had nothing to fear.

But that awful doubt still lingered in the darkest corners of my mind, preying on these convictions and my confidence. Who would—could, or even should—save *me?*

On a brighter note, we made good progress over the next two days—at least, that's what Way said. Apparently, the amount of paperwork for a black-market operation differed from the amount for a perfectly legal one.

That wasn't an exciting discovery.

Thankfully, four o'clock quickly approached, marking the end of Way's workday and the slogging through documents. He'd left to retrieve a few more files before wrapping up. I was colour-coordinating the pens.

When the door opened, I half-expected to see the guard, not Way. Agent Way, however, greeted me.

"Okay, one last thing and this moves from my department," he said.

Freedom! "What's left?" I enquired. How could we be that close?

Way nodded toward the door. "You'll see."

It didn't take long to reach our destination. Way unlocked a door and proceeded inside. I followed.

The room surprised me for a moment. It wasn't because the walls were empty, or because the table in the centre of the brilliantly lit area was covered in notepads and wires snaking to monitors. The surprise came from the window looking into the room next to this one. Beyond the glass, there was another tiny, bright room furnished with a steel table and chair. A man sat chained to the table, staring at the ceiling.

Of a room identical to the one I'd been in.

"What are we doing?" I asked, turning from the man behind the one-way glass back to Way.

"I just need you to tell me who he is," Way said, pointing through the glass. I examined the person I'd initially thought was a stranger. Blood stained his slacks and shoes, while the true colour of his tattered, untucked dress shirt was hidden beneath grime and sweat stains. Muscles bulged within the sleeves, leading to raw, red wrists likely caused by struggling against the handcuffs. Veins popped from his neck as he moved his gaze from the ceiling to his hands. It was then I saw his full facial profile.

My breath caught in my throat, while bitterness and fear burned in my gut. My fist clenched.

"Him." I could practically see the gun in his calloused hands. "He shot the senator." Touching my injured arm, I continued, "He tried to—"

Way's attention quickly dropped to my fingers caressing the bandage. He cut me off. "It's a good thing he's not very good at his job."

I fought the urge to run and looked at the gunman's face again. It was strangely familiar; I had seen it before the gala.

Then it hit me.

"He saw us," I uttered.

Way shook his head. "He can't. This glass is—"

"No," I interrupted. "The day we went to check out the building. He saw us leave."

*And he knew me.* I finished my sentence mentally, recounting a flicker of recognition in his eyes that day.

Way's eyebrows arched in concern. "You're sure?"

"Positive," I said. "Do you know who he is?"

Way stared through the glass. "No ID, no record, and the guy won't talk." He stepped back, as if he remembered saying something similar of me. "But even if we did, you wouldn't be cleared to know."

The man sat perfectly still. My fist clenched harder. "Is that everything?" I asked through a locked jaw. I was done fighting the urge to run. Now the urge to retaliate churned my blood.

"Yes." Way moved to the door and let me slip out. He trailed close behind.

My feet knew where to go. It didn't matter that my mind didn't know where I was; my feet recalled every step back to Way's office.

When we hit my destination, Way didn't open the door. Instead, he led me past it, saying, "You're done for the evening. We'll pick it back up tomorrow."

Way dropped me off in my cell. The door clicked gently behind me. I dug my nails into my palm. I tried to breathe deeply through my nose and analyze the face. I fought to ignore the vile pain in my arm.

He knew me.

I'd kill him.

# CHAPTER NINETEEN

"Forty-five, forty-six," I groaned, pushing my body quickly up from the floor with my good arm, only to bring it down again. Killing anyone wasn't an option now.

Working out was a close second.

I finished my set and looked at my bed. My Bible rested on the pillow from this morning.

It could sit there for a few more reps.

I flipped to my back and began sit-ups, waiting for the time when I'd be tired enough to collapse into sleep.

I stopped counting my sit-ups. The blood in my veins only pumped hotter, but still I brought my torso to my knees. Over. And over. And over.

Finally, I sprawled out on the floor, gasping for air. I closed my eyes. His face was still there.

"Okay," I reasoned with myself, pulling my body toward the bed. "Killing him won't help you figure out why he knows you or why he shot you."

At that, I hurled the pillow across the cell. The book thudded softly against the cot. My bookmark had flown from my Bible, and the Bible itself was resting spine-up.

I sighed, "You don't live that way anymore." My tight-but-tired body crawled onto my cot, and my hands grasped the black book. I curled my knees to my chest and forced my tear-stained eyes to focus on the pages.

Sleep came quickly after that. With sleep came the morning. With the morning came the end of the deal. With the end of the deal came my hasty departure.

And that face would no longer haunt me. On the flip side, I'd never know why he haunted me—why he shot me, why he knew me—in the first place.

Irony.

Soon enough, Way and I were standing outside Richards's office, likely for the last time.

Way gave me a cautious glance. I rolled my shoulders, banishing yesterday's events into the farthest corners of my brain.

I'd be out of here soon.

An agent slipped out of the office, and we slipped in to take his place.

As usual, Way placed our paperwork on the desk. Richards looked it over. They discussed it like I wasn't in the room.

Today, however, would be the last time.

My weight shifted from one foot to the other as they talked. I forced my breathing to be regular, although the rising anticipation of being rid of this place scattered butterflies all through my gut.

Finally, Richards put the paperwork down. "Agent Way, I need to speak with you privately before we can wrap this up," he said.

Way nodded. "Of course, Agent Richards." He cast a questioning glance toward me.

Richards answered his wordless inquiry. "I have a security guard waiting to take Miss Black to your office."

Way moved to open the door. I slid toward the opening but maintained eye contact with Richards.

I spoke. "I take it I'm not leaving today either?"

Richards sighed and folded his hands, "Miss Black, my job is to ensure the safety of the public. I'm afraid I can't let you go, knowing you have information and skills that could protect the innocent and convict the criminal."

It was poetic. However, it sure didn't make sense. Wasn't that what I'd done?

The guard escorted me back to the office.

I sat in my regular spot, resting my head on my hands, and allowed my mind to wander for a few moments.

Then I realized that the guard wasn't going to leave.

Between the events of the last few days and the awkwardness of a security guard watching me do nothing, having my mind wander became a miserable idea. I reached across the desk for a pen and a page. The pen touched the surface and so began my list:

*Face tanned and dark.*

*Nose straight but small for his head.*

*Height around two metres.*

*Medium build.*

*Eyes are—*

I paused. His eyes were different. The man who fired the shot had brown eyes, surrounded by creases. They made his younger body look old and worn, yet they smiled with his lips as he took the shot on me.

He was a living nightmare.

I directed my attention back to the page. A not-so-friendly blob of ink scooshed all across my list.

I crumpled the page, chucked it in the trash with razor-sharp precision, leaned back, and closed my eyes. I could have sworn I sensed the guard behind me grin, intensifying the awkwardness of the situation.

Regardless, I pleaded with my mind to remember where I could possibly know this man from.

Nothing.

Instead, my mind reverted to other topics. My family and the nightmares that accompanied them was one. Each horrible dream had a similar message: my family would die while I watched, doing nothing to save them.

I fought the urge to physically shake that thought out of my head, trying to replace it with mental images of what my new life would look like. I could grow my hair out again and find a job at a quiet coffee shop somewhere until I had a new direction. I could go to university for a degree I'd never previously entertained. I could…

Hope and pray that Way and Richards would be done soon.

Finally, Way marched through the door. "Grab your coat," he commanded.

"What's going on?"

Way continued. "You'll see. One thing we are gonna do is stop by the laundromat, so you'll need your bag."

I raised an eyebrow. He shrugged and said, "Are you really gonna argue that one?" Way glanced down at his desk, noticing that I had subconsciously straightened it while he'd been gone (including colour-coordinating his pens). "The boss cleared it, and you have nothing better to do."

I cautiously moved to my feet. My hand fingered the bandage on my arm as I said, "What about…"

Way dangled keys between his fingers. "His buddy can't hurt you if he doesn't recognize you."

# CHAPTER TWENTY

It wasn't surprising to an ex-assassin that the FBI had a huge arsenal of disguises for every possible scenario. I'd examined a number of them on the afternoon of the gala. However, seeing said ex-assassin in a blonde wig and sweats was surprising, both to the agent and the woman wearing them.

The game of dress-up didn't stop there, however. Way replaced his dress pants with ripped jeans and his spiky hairdo for a worn leather jacket and slicked-back look.

"Better?" Way motioned head-to-toe, pausing at the place where my injured arm had been cleaned and re-wrapped. A flowy grey sleeve covered the bandage.

I dropped shades over my eyes. "I guess we'll find out," I said with a shrug.

We hit the sidewalk. The sun reflected off the multitude of windshields flooding the busy street. The jostling pedestrians were far more preoccupied with their phones and bus schedules to note the pair of young adults emerging from the FBI building.

"See?" Way nudged.

I withheld my response.

"This'll be good." He smiled, squinting at the buildings around us until his eyes could adjust.

This was the sixth time he'd assured me of such. As exciting as the outing was, I was still unsure about the safety and practicality of the trip. The motive was also baffling.

Three minutes into our walk, Way turned abruptly to the right. A tacky orange and blue sign greeted us. A sarcastic, "Wow," escaped my lips.

"Inside is better," Way coaxed.

He waltzed through the glass door. It was painful to admit that he was right. The orange theme continued through the foyer area, varying into shades of yellow and green. The space was divided into several sections, each holding different types of chrome-plated equipment. Although the gaudy colouring of the space made its appearance dubious, the building demonstrated the care that went into cleanliness. The smell of disinfectant clung faintly to the air as fans attempted to blow fresh oxygen into the gym. Weights, treadmills, and other machinery that I'd never seen before gleamed through the foyer windows.

My body ached at the sight of them, reminding me of last night's workout. My mind, however, sparked with enthusiasm.

"Jamie!" an older gent exclaimed from behind the counter. He flashed a confident grin at me and strode forward.

"I need a favour," Way said as he grasped the man's muscular hand. "My friend's new around here. I have an errand to run across town. Could you…"

"Definitely! A friend of yours is a friend of mine." The man smiled, smacking the counter enthusiastically. The engraved lettering on a metal-plated name tag read, "Donny."

Way flipped out his wallet and pulled out the appropriate green bills. "There." Way turned to me. "You gonna be okay?"

I nodded, still starry-eyed at the array of workout equipment.

"Perfect! I'll see you soon, Susanne." Way smiled.

"Thanks."

He reached for my backpack full of laundry. I must have looked skeptical because he whispered, "I'll take care of it."

With that, he waved at Donny and disappeared onto the street.

"All right, Missy Susie." Donny reached behind the desk and handed me a pass card and a towel. "Change rooms and showers that way, and from there you'll see a door right into the gym." Donny pointed with a crooked finger.

"Tha—"

Donny continued. "Let me know if you have any questions. Any questions at all."

"Yes s—"

"I'm happy to help you with any of the equipment as well," Donny offered. How did Way ever have a conversation with this guy?

"Thanks!" I blurted, nodding gracefully to cover up the "blurt." My feet quickly shuffled into the change room and onward into the gym.

It didn't take me long to figure out the equipment, nor to break a good sweat. My muscles burned. My breathing strengthened. The stress of the last few weeks melted away.

My body felt good, my emotions simplified, and my heart recharged.

"Thank you, Jesus," I whispered as I stretched. Twisting myself into a knot, I happily noted that my flexibility hadn't changed during the last few weeks.

Steps clicked on the polished floor behind me.

A whistle followed. "That's impressive."

I turned, simultaneously unweaving my arms from my legs. "Can't you do that?"

Way leaned back on an elliptical machine, swinging my backpack on his forearm. "Can't say I've ever tried." Way tossed the bag beside me. I detected a slight whiff of fabric softener. "How was it?" the agent asked.

"Good." I stood, shaking out my arms. "I'll be back." Scooping up the bag, I slipped by Way and into the change room.

As I stepped into the shower area, a renewed excitement filled my chest; I hadn't realized how much I missed being consistently clean, especially after a hard workout. The daily routine of rinsing off with paper towels and tap water could only do so much for so long.

Needless to say, the cascading hot water was a satisfying end to the little vacation from my FBI day job. Having my own clean laundry topped off the escapade wonderfully.

Slipping the wig back over my own short, black hair, I checked myself in the mirror. For a split second, I looked like anyone else. No one would suspect that I'd been involved in preventing a political assassination, or that the bandage on my arm covered a tender bullet wound.

The energized feeling in my chest wiggled its way up into my face, boosting the corners of my lips into a smile. In the last few weeks I'd gone from sinner to saved, dying to living, from dirty to clean, and—apparently—from black to blonde.

"Blonde's not bad," Way tilted his head as I approached him in the foyer.

"Not my preference," I countered, "But I'll survive a few more minutes."

Way quipped, "That's not very long," as he stepped toward the door.

"Aren't we going back to the office?

"Nope. No more work to do," he replied over his shoulder.

I raised an eyebrow. Didn't I have work to do? Wasn't that why I couldn't leave?

Soon enough, we sat in a rustic wooden booth at the café we'd been in the week before, eating burgers and drinking lattes amid autumn decor.

Way had fully bounced back into his regular charm mode.

I wasn't entirely sold that food and relaxation were the only reasons we were here. Personal experience taught me that one could purposefully hide something by distracting someone else with food. The difference was that I'd used sandwiches with Tyson, not burgers.

"Do you come here often?" I said, picking a pickle off my burger. Was I beating around the bush? Yes. Did I care? Clearly not that much.

Way worked through a large bite. "Beats packing a lunch," he shrugged.

I nodded. Not a direct answer. New question. "Did you grow up around here?"

"Naw." Way swallowed. "My dad was in the military. We moved a lot." He straightened his posture as if his back had suddenly tensed.

A minuscule crack had appeared in his persona. I pushed. "Your mom was a professor, right? I'm sure that dynamic was fun."

Way rolled his eyes. "Oh yeah, loads of fun. You learn quick." His tone was superficially light.

"Did that inspire you to work in the FBI?" I asked, adding a quirky smile.

"It was the best of both worlds—education and physical discipline." Way sipped his latte. Once again, he danced around a straight answer.

He beat me to ask the next question. "More salt?" He pushed the shaker my way.

I set the shaker aside. "I'm trying to imagine a young, aspiring James Way." I tapped my finger on my chin. "At least, I assume you were young once."

"You assume wrongly," Way matched my remark. "I've always been this fantastically grown up." Something in his tone signalled a touch of truth in that statement.

Both of us had finished our burgers. Way pushed against the table. "Free time is over. Back to the office."

Way held the wooden café door open for me as we left, greeted by the chilly autumn breeze.

My feet took a tight left turn. My shoulder collided with a man just outside the door.

"Excuse me," he grumbled, hardly missing a step. Way came up beside me, quipping something about how unlike me it was to not check my surroundings before proceeding.

I focused on the man who struggled to disappear among the crowd. In his distinctly faded and worn-out black jacket, however, he made himself an easily traceable target.

"Security," I muttered, reading the lettering across his back and scouring my brain for an elusive association.

Way whispered in my ear, "Is it an assassin thing to stare conspicuously for long periods of time at men," he teased, "or is that just a girl thing?"

"We use our peripheral," I answered absently. The man glanced back, revealing his profile.

Revealing his identity.

"Gotta move." I grasped Way's arm and walked in the other direction.

"Sadie, that man didn't recognize—" Way started to say.

"You have no idea who that man is," I replied, keeping my pace steady. My heartbeat didn't follow suit.

"Do I need to apprehend someone?" he said lightly. His eyebrows arched in confusion.

"I need to see Richards."

"Why?" Way asked.

I closed my eyes and confirmed the face, linking it to the one I'd seen just a day earlier.

I exhaled. "I know who our suspect is."

# CHAPTER TWENTY-ONE

Richards's office was becoming strangely familiar.

Way seemed to think similarly.

"She claims to have information, sir," Way said dryly. I hadn't had opportunity to explain the whole who-what-when-why of the situation, and he wasn't convinced that I actually had all those answers.

From what I'd said on the way here, he must have thought I was crazy.

Richards looked me over, then turned back to Way. "Concerning what?"

I jumped in. "Names and locations."

Richards placed a hand briefly on his chin. "Wait outside," he said curtly, directing the command at Way.

Way's jaw dropped slightly. I could practically hear him mentally objecting to this arrangement, but instead he nodded and complied. Richards motioned to a chair and pushed a paper toward the edge of his desk.

"What names and why do I care?" he questioned abruptly.

"The name is Thomas Raleigh, owner of Raleigh Technologies," I replied, simultaneously scribbling down the information. "And at least two of his security guards were present at the gala. One called the shots. The other fired the gun."

"Names of the guards?"

"If I had those, I would have started with them," I said, spinning the page and making eye contact.

"Where's the evidence?" Richards pushed.

"Not in my possession," I admitted.

"That doesn't help me, Black."

"*You* have one of them in custody," I returned.

"Where is Raleigh?"

I paused for only a moment. "Dead, sir."

"Why associate the guards with a dead man?" Richards probed. His tone grew more intense.

"Because I'm the reason he's dead." The words left my mouth naturally. It was just another fact.

I could see the neurons firing in his brain, but his eyes never left mine. His voice dropped, "Do they know who you are?"

"Probably not 'who,' but they know I fired the gun," I responded.

"That explains it." Richards opened the filing cabinet under his desk and pulled out a bulging folder. On top were my witness report and theory.

"Explains what?" I asked in vain.

Richards raised his voice. "Way, get in here!"

The door opened a crack. "Yes sir?" A voice addressed Richards. I turned. Way was clearly pleased to be needed.

"Sit down," Richards directed, not impressed. He picked up the page and handed it to Way. "We have a lead on the second suspect."

Way cocked an eyebrow. "You believe her?"

I couldn't quite figure out what made my story so far-fetched. You'd think Way would know me better by now.

"We have a possible motivation for our current suspect's one shot," Richards stated, ignoring Way's question. Way made eye contact expectantly.

"Which is?" he urged Richards to continue.

"She killed his employer." Richards pointed at me and the bandage on my arm. Way glanced at my arm and then my face for confirmation. That was the fragment of the story I'd neglected to share with him. I nodded.

"She was shot out of spite, not necessity," Way said, processing the information and its consequences.

"Theoretically, yes." Richards tilted his head.

"What about the senator?" Way asked, as if I'd somehow vanished.

"Raleigh Technologies is a large corporation. A Senate investigation on white-collar crime could be a threat," Richards reasoned.

"Raleigh sold more than electronics," I added, remembering the papers I'd found in his safe. Perhaps my snooping had been beneficial.

Way cocked his head. "What's that supposed to mean?"

"He was involved in human trafficking."

Richards leaned back to digest. "We can all make up information, Miss Black. Where's the proof?"

Was the idea that far-fetched? "It's in his safe, at his private address," I clarified.

Richards nodded after some thought. "Well then, an investigation would really be troublesome."

"That would be a concrete motivation for the assassination attempt," Way concluded.

"This'll get us much farther with the suspect." Richards reached out for the page. As Way returned it, Richards asked me, "Is there anything else of pertinence that you recall?"

"No sir," I said. "But your next suspect is still in D.C."

Richards looked over his non-existent glasses. "Can you describe him?"

"Same man from the report."

"Excellent," Richards said. "Good work, Black. Looks like we have more to do." A quick glance at Way revealed that he wasn't as impressed as his boss.

The senior agent gave another non-verbal cue to leave. I pivoted to the door, only to turn back again.

"Sir, I'm more useful to you alive than dead when it comes to information. If anyone else knows I'm here, the second option will become reality," I told him.

Richards's features softened pensively. "I'll see what can be arranged."

We left the office and headed for the office.

"So you still don't like the FBI life," Way said playfully as we walked. I'd learned from experience, however, that "playful" was just another way to collect information.

I chose my words carefully. "I can't help but feel that I'm not getting the full experience."

Way glanced from the corner of an eye. "You don't have clearance for the full experience," he remarked offhandedly.

"I can't judge what I don't know," I observed.

"But you can judge what you do know. And because of Agent Richards, that knowledge is probably higher than your clearance level."

What was that supposed to mean? "My whole life has been above the 'clearance level,'" I retorted. "A lot higher than yours."

Way wasn't finished. "I'm not convinced."

"Come again?" I asked. What was he suggesting?

"I've worked with other agents with a similar clearance level to Richards. Only Richards was willing to take your case. The others held views similar to my own. He's also given you more information than any intern gets, let alone a criminal, and he bargained for your freedom."

"And…" I coaxed. He wasn't telling me everything. One would think I'd be used to that by now.

Way stopped and stared straight into my eyes. "You are a woman of facts. Doesn't that coincidence strike you as odd?"

He had a point. Something was off. I wouldn't let him know that, though. "What you call odd I call provision." I continued walking.

Way grabbed my shoulders. "If provision is the case, then why are you leaving?"

"Provision released me."

"And I could say it's kept you here. You're the Christian. Maybe this was God's provision," Way volleyed in return, gesturing to the walls around us.

I glared up at his tall stature. "That's twisting what I said."

"Yet you don't deny it." Way stepped back. A smug grin lifted his lips. In his mind, he'd won. It was no more than a game.

It still meant I'd lost. I shook it off and fired my last comment: "Whatever lets you sleep at night."

"At least I sleep." He turned. His stride lengthened, snatching away whatever victory I'd had.

Mine quickened while my mind chewed on what Way had said. What if he had a point? Why would God keep me here? And how did Way know about my lack of sleep?

I fought a shudder as we entered the office. The images and emotions of my nightmares coursed through my mind and body.

Way mindlessly opened his desk drawer. He picked up a file, peeked inside it, and quickly thrust it back into its hiding place.

Odd. "What's that?" I asked.

He shrugged off his haste. "The file for finding those responsible for the assassination attempt."

I cocked my head. "Guess I saved us some work." I smirked.

Way didn't return it.

Dryness seized my lips and tongue, while I swallowed whatever moisture was left between my arid gums. "It wasn't for Raleigh's guys, was it?"

He closed the drawer slowly, answering my question.

I pushed my palms into his oak desk. "They didn't fire any shots. They left no evidence. There was no attempt."

Way ran his hand through his hair. "You reported them, Black. We have to investigate."

I took a step back. I sat down. I tried to control whatever emotion was building tension in my chest. I tried to forget about the "death penalty" poster in my old home, or the fact that my family was far more vulnerable than I cared to admit.

Because of me.

"So, were you going to tell me?" I asked quietly, "Or take me out for lunches until I spilled everything you needed to know?"

Silence.

# CHAPTER TWENTY-TWO

Tears. I hated tears.

At the same time, tears were the only thing that always did what they promised to do. They came when you were sad. They were pulled down by gravity. They left salty streaks wherever they went. Inevitably, they caused your nose to get stuffy and runny. Tears always delivered.

I flung my backpack on the cot, grasping my Bible from its place on the pillow. I opened the pages, determinedly seeking a distraction. My bookmark took me to Revelation—a captivating book, to say the least—and I read from Chapter 21. It said so much about life and about being new, but the tension in my shoulders wouldn't leave.

Then, the encouraging content of the passage shifted grimly. My eyes resorted to skimming at this point, trying to get back to the lighter side of things. Unfortunately, Verse 8 refused to be ignored: "…murderers…shall have their part in the lake which burns with fire and brimstone, which is the second death."

I nearly hurled the book.

Yes, the second death was no longer a threat to this murderer. The Bible made it exceedingly clear that Jesus had paid that penalty on the cross and had graciously given me new life. I was free and I was saved…but my family wasn't either of those things. Instead, they all lived unaware of the ultimate consequences of their actions, unable to commit to a God that they knew nothing about and destined for a death beyond their imaginations.

If only they knew.

A thought itched at the edge of my brain. The face and name of someone who could tell them of "the second death" and how to avoid it appeared clearly in my mind's eye.

Considering her betrayal, they likely wouldn't listen to her.

Concerning her current role as an FBI informant, they likely wouldn't trust her.

Recognizing the dire threat that finding them would present to her own life, I just didn't think she would do it.

I really couldn't blame her.

I flipped passages, tormented by the reality that these pages held. "God, You have to send someone else," I pleaded. The pain of further tears pricked at the back of my eyeballs. Completely drained and exhausted, I placed the book on the floor and rolled onto my cot. Despite the fact that it was mid-afternoon, I would sleep. Sleep was better than this.

~~

I was back home. My family and I sat around the table, feasting. It was loud. It was bright. It was normal.

Dad held up a glass for a toast. I breathed in, preparing for Dad's words of encouragement and challenge. That breath was interrupted by a sharp, gut-retching smell resembling concentrated bleach. I scanned the room. My father, mother, and brothers all had a clear liquid in their wine glasses, while mine was empty.

Chlorine? Chloric acid?

Whatever was causing the smell was in their glasses, and no one else seemed to know or care.

Dad's voice slowed as he ended his speech and lifted the glass to his mouth. My family followed suit.

I attempted lifting my feet. For the first time in one of these dreams, I was able to move.

The worst part was…I didn't.

I felt a tear slide down my face—my real face—as I watched my family cheerfully slam back the poisonous substance. I woke up to its cold memory.

It was too real.

More tears flowed down my face, silently. I didn't scream. I didn't bawl.

I just cried with no sound.

"Why couldn't I have knocked it from his hands?" I screeched through silent sobs. "Even if the acid would have splashed and burned him, or me, it wouldn't have been lethal. I could have…"

Said something.

# CHAPTER TWENTY-THREE

The guard dropped me off at Way's office. Two takeout cups of specialty coffee topped with swirly whipped cream and caramel sauce, partnered with a small chocolate bar, held down a desk covered with papers and file folders. A single tablet sat among the chaos, shadowed by Way's hunched figure.

The pens were not colour-coordinated.

I wasn't going to mention it.

I wrapped my cold hands around the coffee cup and slid down the wall to the floor. My knees met my chest, and I sipped.

"You realize you can sit on a chair."

"I'd hate for it to be above my clearance," I responded.

Way's eyes moved from the tablet to the full-grown woman sulking silently on his floor. I kept my eyes trained on my cup, although I could see a tinge of regret in his body language.

"How long have you been searching for them?" I asked plainly.

Way sighed. "Saturday night."

I grasped the coffee cup tighter, pushing my sneakered heels into the floor. It was Thursday.

Way opened his mouth to continue. "We don't have any leads—"

The phone interrupted. Way hesitated before picking it up.

I focused on the intricacies of the caramel-to-whipped-cream ratio, although I recognized Richards's voice through the phone.

Way hung up. "Richards wants you," he said. We stepped out of the office into a very different world than had been there when I'd left my cell fifteen minutes ago.

The J. Edgar Hoover Building buzzed—literally. The humming of machines and tapping of shoes up and down the halls reminded me of the hum of a beehive. This hive, however, had been attacked.

At least, it buzzed until the worker bees saw me. Then it froze.

Way nodded cordially at his co-workers as we weaved past the agents and through the halls.

Richards and Martin both stood in Richards's office. "Glad you could join us," Richards said. The lack of a smile told me otherwise.

Richards held up a transparent plastic bag with a note inside. "Explain this," he commanded, shoving it into my hand. Way peered over my shoulder. The yellow page read:

*To they who hold she who Sews,*
*Be sure that the dark Archer knows.*

*His shot is sure; his Torch is lit,*
*And the Storm he brings will not quit.*
*That which Computes is not dim;*
*The Fate you await is rather grim.*
*Be she held by own or by you,*
*Step back or we'll step through.*

My fingers caressed my hair, remembering the locks that had once been there.

Way snatched the bag from me. "It's a threat."

"It's tradition," I muttered. My grandmother would have been proud.

Way didn't hear me. "When did it come in?"

Richards nodded toward the note. "That was posted at the main entrance this morning."

"You have video on it?" Way flipped the bag to see the blank back of the page.

"The only evidence we have is of a young child putting it on the door." Richards gripped his solid wood desk, threatening to snap it in two. "Nothing else." He looked at me. "Except her."

How much information did they have on me?

Way raised an eyebrow at me. "This makes sense to you?"

I nodded, pointing to the top line. "This references my call name during jobs."

"And the other lines?" Way asked.

"My family's call names."

Silence dominated the room. Way processed. Richards studied me, as if I had more information I was withholding. Martin was simply stoic.

I was sewing pieces together.

Way sighed, "Well, this could make finding them easier."

"Oh yeah, because threats have always been an ideal means of locating people," I said sarcastically, continuing my thought process.

Martin cleared his throat and parted his concrete lips. "You're telling me you've been looking for them, and they march right up and put a notice on the FBI's front door?" His eyes moved from Richards to me.

Richards stepped forward. "It switched to Agent Way's department yesterday. There is no way—"

"That a family of wanted criminals could have posted a note on the door of the grand J. Edgar Hoover Building in Washington, D.C.—whose security I need not remind you of—and not be caught without the helping hand of an insider," Martin finished.

What Martin didn't understand was that the FBI were always playing defence. My family excelled at offence.

I excelled at offence.

We'd just have to flip the game.

"We need to limit their ability to attack," I said.

Richards raised his eyebrows. "You are quite safe in here, Miss Black."

Martin straightened his shoulders and spoke. "It's not the criminal's safety that I'm concerned about."

"Listen, I have—" I started to say.

"Richards," Martin interrupted sternly, "she needs to leave."

Richards looked at Way. "Please take her out of the office. Agent Martin and I have some details to discuss."

Way and I stood out in the hall. People buzzed and breezed by us.

My face flushed. To someone who had always worked behind the scenes, this felt like an overwhelming amount of attention.

Finally, Richards summoned us back in. Martin had a smug look illuminating his face.

"Miss Black, I am arranging for you to leave as soon as possible under witness protection. You have been suspended from any paperwork that you may have been working on, and you will from now on act strictly as a witness," Richards said dryly. "We appreciate and commend your work here."

Martin's smug look shifted slightly, evidently disagreeing with the final statement.

Way and I were dismissed.

"What's next?" I asked. We worked our way back to Way's office. The halls still felt busy, although now fewer people travelled them.

"Well," Way began, "I guess you get to sit in my office. I'll get a phone call, and I'll take you over to the witness protection division."

"Then?" I dug deeper.

"Then you'll be sent somewhere, be given a new name and a job, and we'll only bug you if we need you."

I chuckled. "So, I should get a call in the next couple of days."

"Ha," said Way. "We were doing fine without you, Miss Black."

We approached his office. "Will I be in here a long time?" I asked him.

Way pointed to his office questioningly and raised his eyebrows. "It depends on where the department is at today."

"Could I grab my things, then?" I requested, thinking that sitting there but having little to do with current circumstances would be overwhelmingly frustrating.

Way shrugged. "Sure."

At the cell, I realized how much my few possessions had managed to overrun the space. Despite that fact, I had packed my things back in my bag in two minutes and thirteen seconds.

Way leaned against the doorframe. "Ready?"

I glanced around the bland room out of habit, as if the cot, pillow, and toilet would have concealed my belongings the first time.

"Yes," I confirmed.

"You'll likely be back tonight. It depends—"

"On the department. I know," I finished. "I guess I'm just optimistic."

~~

Using my bag of clothes as a cushion made the floor a much more comfortable sitting space. I'd had to manoeuvre the hairbrush to a spot where it wasn't digging into my spine, but other than that, it was a perfectly suitable way to relax, recline, and spend my final moments at FBI headquarters. The Bible on my lap fell open while I nestled against the bag and the wall. Instinctively, I reached for the bookmark and pulled those pages apart, drowning out Way's fingers tapping at his keyboard.

Revelation 21 greeted me again: "He who overcomes shall inherit all things, and I will be his God and he shall be My son. But…murderers…shall have their part in the lake…"

I instinctively flipped the pages somewhere else. John 8:32 was much more pleasant: "And you shall know the truth, and the truth shall make you free."

Free. I had been set free in many ways.

Yet, there was a feeling in my gut—not nervousness, not apprehension, not indigestion—but a feeling that I was missing something.

Like the feeling I'd had on my last job with my family.

I read the verse again, going a bit beyond it for context. The passage was clear.

My conscience wasn't.

"You really want me to tell them, don't you?" I addressed Jesus in my thoughts.

I looked back at the page. "And you shall know the truth…" it read. Scripture had answered my question.

I put my head in my hands. "You don't get it, Jesus. They'll kill me," I whispered softly.

Silence followed.

Reality sunk in.

I sighed and proceeded to speak in my mind. "They killed You. But You came anyway."

Slightly aware that Way was only an arm's length away, I confirmed my direction silently, praying, "Okay. If this is where You want me, then You'll have to help me."

I opened my eyes and tilted my head back against the wall. While a fear factor remained in my brain, my shoulders relaxed and that strange feeling inside me changed into peace.

It was like I could breathe fully again.

The phone startled the breath out of me, which was an impressive feat given my previous occupation. Way casually picked up the phone. This time, I couldn't hear the other voice. All I caught was Way's, "Yes sir. I'll take her."

Way hung up.

"I can't go yet."

Way turned to look down at me seated on the floor. "What?"

"I can't go yet," I repeated emphatically. "It's my family."

"That's why you're leaving, remember? Richards's deal, your freedom, Martin's complaint…"

My Bible found its place on the top of the bag, and I stood. I locked my gaze, allowing my eyes to state with finality, "I'm not backing down."

Way also rose, straightening his tie and sleeves. "Well, looks like you'll have to figure out how that's going to work. That was the department head."

As we weaved through the halls, I stepped out in front of Way. I knew where Richards's office was.

Way said something behind me. I didn't register it, however. I stayed my course.

He repeated it. No response from me.

"Sadie!" Way shouted firmly. I spun. He hadn't called me by my first name before.

Way gestured the other direction with his thumb. That department was in a separate wing.

I looked back. "I have to see Richards," I said. There wasn't another option.

"Not my problem," Way responded.

"Not your choice," I retorted. Couldn't he just listen?

I resumed my original course and kept walking.

"Do you have information?" Way called from behind me.

"What?" I pivoted my head slightly, but my legs didn't stop.

Way's dress shoes slapped against the floor as he jogged to catch up to me, sending his bright tie bouncing against his chest. His voice dropped to a whisper. "Do you have any more information to bargain with?"

"Not explicitly."

"But you have something?" Way probed.

"Yes."

"That will help find the attempted assassins, including your family?"

"Yes."

Way's face revealed a mental debate. Was he going to try to stop me or assist me? He had an opportunity to get rid of me. Would he really give that away?

A small sigh escaped his lips. "I guess I have some work to do."

"Why?"

Way put his hand on my shoulders and propelled me back down the hall toward the witness protection department. "You still need to go to this meeting. When we close the case, it'll be one less hoop to jump through."

"What about Rich—" I started.

"This case is mine. You have information I need. You stay."

# CHAPTER TWENTY-FOUR

Pain throbbed in my arm, shooting bursts of discomfort through my shoulder. I adjusted my shoulder to decrease the pain, only to discover it had fallen asleep.

A click pulsed from the door. I jerked up from the desk.

"Well, good morning, sleepyhead," Way smirked, holding a cup of steaming coffee in each hand. He placed one on the desk right beside a scribbled note, reading:

*For when you wake up:*

*I went home. I'll see you first thing in the morning. (Yes, the door is locked. Yes, those jackets are in case you decide to sleep on the floor instead of the desk.)*

*—J. Way*

The clock read 8:30 a.m. Way's tie and shirt were distinctly different shades of blue than when I'd seen him last.

Wasn't that just a few moments ago?

Way pushed the coffee toward me. "Here, it's leaded. It'll help." I must have looked as dazed as I felt because he continued. "You fell asleep."

That fact finally clicked in my fog-filled brain. "Oh yeah." I sat up. "Of course."

I tried to recall the night before. I'd had my meeting. Way had then contacted Richards and explained the need for me to stay another few days. Richards's only stipulation was that he expected a report and plan by this morning. We figured out the best way, considering circumstances, to arrange a meeting with my family. In doing so, we also discovered a serious loose end that Richards should know about. Then I was extremely tired. Way left the office to access and gather more data, and...

No more memory after that.

Way slipped a dry bran muffin beside the coffee.

"Oh, thanks," I mumbled.

"No problem."

I blinked three times. I must have been really out of it, because my thoughts were still out of place.

"So, where did we leave off?" I asked, sipping the hot caffeine and turning to the computer. Way tilted the monitor for me to see.

"We're done." He hit the print key while I scanned our plan on the screen. Some parts weren't clear to me, but that was attributable to my grogginess. I nodded.

"You're confident?" I asked, breaking off a bite-sized chunk of the muffin.

"Well, no. It's still a long shot, but it's enough information to make your case. Richards is still on your side, and, well, it's out of state, so it won't put the FBI HQ in further danger. It also has essential information on where one could find, and thus trap, your family. It postpones your leaving, thereby giving greater opportunity to see your family, plus you get extra brownie points for reporting this to the FBI. It's the best shot you have."

"Sounds perfect." I slipped the muffin into my mouth and brought the paper coffee cup to my lips to chase it down.

Way placed the pages in a folder, double-checking that they were printed correctly and in order. I finished my snack of a breakfast.

It was a matter of moments until we stood outside Richards's door. A small opening between the door and its frame allowed the sound of frustrated, one-sided conversation to make its way into the bustling hall. Way tapped my arm and mouthed, "Let's come back."

I shook my head in protest. Richards must have detected our movement because his voice softened.

I peeked through the crack, and Richards waved us in. Obviously, the conversation wasn't horribly confidential, as he continued listening to the voice on the other side of the phone. He pointed and tapped to his empty desk.

Way stepped forward and placed the file—my bargaining chip—on said desk.

I followed him and immediately snatched the folder back. I wasn't just casually giving away this chance at finding my family. Way cast me a sideways glance, hinting that I ought to replace it. My eyebrows lifted and blue eyes widened to wordlessly declare, "Nope."

Richards caught the silent conversation happening and wrapped up his phone call. "Yes, we will be in further contact. Thank you." He hung up the phone and motioned to the report in my hand.

"Sir, before I hand this to you, I want it to be clear that it comes with a request," I said in a futile attempt to be diplomatic. The breathiness of my voice was far more needy than I'd anticipated.

"Which is?" Richards folded his hands semi-patiently.

"I want to speak with my family before any attempt to arrest is to be made, if such a situation arises," I said, my voice much firmer this time. The plan called for not seeing them at all, but one had to be both resolute and careful when playing with fire.

Richards smiled. "Miss Black, that is a small price to ask for the information you hold in your hands."

"I want it in writing," I said, standing my ground.

Richards's smile deepened—almost a look of pride, but not quite. Richards seemed far more concerned about the meeting with my family than whatever I had to do in exchange for it.

We confirmed it in writing.

I gave Richards the file. He pulled out our report and scanned it.

"Ben and Katherine Monroe, huh?" Richards reacted to the document.

"Yes. I stayed with them, making them a breach of my family's security. Enough of a breach to warrant an attack."

"Or to use as hostages," Richards continued reading.

"Exactly," I nodded. "Before the note on the FBI's door, I was confident they'd be fine. I didn't give it a second thought. Now—"

"You know better." Richards interrupted, shaking his head. "Could have saved me a big headache if you'd drawn this conclusion before, Miss Black." The senior agent turned the page. "And I can't just call the local police department because—"

"Less people. Less mess," Way interjected.

Richards set the document on the desk. "I couldn't agree more."

Part of me rejoiced in his ready agreement, but another part told me that it had come too easily.

Richards thought it through further. "No one else should be involved. We'll take care of it."

We transformed the plan from paper into reality. It wasn't complex. Richards assured us this would be a straightforward trip. We'd fly to the church, pick up the pastor couple, and return to D.C. If anything went wrong, he'd rely on me, as the insider, to beat my family.

Meanwhile, I had the slightly more complex task of settling my mental debate. One part of me hoped that we wouldn't cross paths with the Black clan, but that I could somehow get such a meeting arranged for another time when Ben and Katherine wouldn't be caught in any potential crossfire. The other part of me knew that while running into them was a small possibility, chance was an easily manipulated factor in the hand of God. My recent life experience had proven that much. I had a responsibility to speak with my family about the very reason they'd try to kill me, regardless of other circumstances, and I didn't have a say in when or how the opportunity would arise.

I'd be a fool if I wasn't ready for it.

# CHAPTER TWENTY-FIVE

As awful as it was to think about, my family could really have done an abundance of damage over the years if it had possessed the resources the FBI did. In the space of an hour, we'd received legal permission to abduct a member of the clergy and their spouse, local law enforcement was informed of our operation, and we'd boarded a small, private jet. The preparation behind our scheme, although appearing sketchy, was thorough. The others on the aircraft—namely, Richards and Way—were trained to handle these seemingly improvised circumstances.

Yet I was on board because the FBI didn't really know what to expect, assuming my family showed up.

Not a comforting thought.

On the flip side, the world below (at least, what I could see of it) plastered itself with hues of red and yellow. Cities of grey interrupted the fall colours, sticking out like rifles on the wooden kitchen table. The clouds shifted in varying shades of white. The world fit together so nicely, seamed together by landscapes and connected by winding roads. Was this what God always saw?

My Bible would have been nice company. The muted hum of the jet engines added far more to the ride than our conversations did. Richards sat closer to the front of the plane, bobbing into the cockpit once in a while. Way reclined in a row of seats to my left. A gossip magazine lay sprawled across his lap, although his body language told me he wasn't concerned about what the newest celebrity was wearing. Aside from the pilot and co-pilot, this was our crew.

For the seventh time since takeoff, I mentally tracked through the plan. Arrive at local FBI office. Drive one of their undercover vehicles to the Monroes' church/house. Knock. Flash badges and smiles. Ask nicely. Apologize for inconvenience. Take them to FBI office. Fly back to D.C.

Small crew, simple plan.

We dropped our altitude, growing nearer to the target.

I tilted my head slowly from side-to-side and closed my eyes in a vain attempt to relieve tension. "Relax," I commanded as I exhaled. My fingers firmly massaged just behind my ears, soothing my unsuspecting ear canals as the air pressure in the cabin changed.

We landed. Richards and Way flashed badges, awkwardly pointing back at me.

Richards escorted me into the barred back seat of a black, bulletproof SUV and climbed behind the steering wheel. Way plopped beside him and slid the seat back to accommodate his long legs, leaving me and my squished knees to wonder if informants ever rode shotgun. Another armoured vehicle full of local agents pulled up behind us.

The silence within our vehicle complemented the flakes of snow dancing to the ground, signalling an early winter. No discussion occurred—talking about our plan wouldn't aid the follow-through of that plan.

Richards parked down the street from the church. I positioned a comms unit in my ear as Way slipped out of the vehicle.

My door clicked as Way pulled it open. "This'll be easy," he assured me. Strangely, Way seemed to direct the statement toward himself more than anyone. He was just the law enforcement in this operation. I was the persuasion.

What did *he* have to lose?

My feet moved quickly, eager to finish this. The less time we were on the field of operations, the less likely Pastor Ben and Katherine were to get hurt.

We reached the church and tried the door handle. I wasn't sure whether they'd be there or at home, but the handle gave way, leading Way and I inside.

"Pastor Ben?" I called, jogging toward his office. My pulse quickened as I realized that he wasn't there.

"Where else would he be?" Way wondered aloud, striding into Ben's office like it was his own.

"Kitchen?"

Turning down the hall, I caught the faint sound of a toilet flushing and water running.

The men's room door creaked open and Pastor Ben appeared. "Can I help you?" he asked cordially, making eye contact with Way. His eyes widened as he turned slightly and took in the sight of…well, me.

I glanced at Way. How could I phrase this?

Way slid his hand into his pocket, reaching for his badge.

"Pastor Ben, I need you to come with us," I started to say, then stumbled through a somewhat-rehearsed explanation of why the girl who'd hidden under their roof had pushed them in front of a gun—and not just in a metaphorical sense. Way flashed his badge a few times, solidifying my testimony.

The pastor's facial expressions probably would have been entertaining if the circumstances weren't literally life-or-death.

"I'm really sorry," my voice cracked weakly as I finished.

The pastor was speechless. I couldn't blame him.

"Is Katherine here?" I redirected my attention to preventing further damage rather than dwelling on what I'd already done.

"She's at home, having a Bible study," the pastor answered absent-mindedly. "May I just have a moment?"

I nodded.

Pastor Ben scurried into his office, leaving Way and I in the hall. I turned away, pretending to look at the crayon-coloured decorations that lined the walls while biting back stubborn tears. Way's voice came through the comms unit, requesting the go-ahead to walk the pastor across the street to his house rather than shuttling him in the SUV. Given the fact that our operation was to go unnoticed, Richards obliged.

"I'm ready." Pastor Ben stood in the doorway to his office with his jacket and a bulging briefcase. I peeked past him to see the very spot I'd occupied when he and Katherine first shared about Jesus with me.

If only they had known.

"I wouldn't change it." Pastor Ben broke my trance, reading my mind. I watched a tear form in the corner of his eye. "I wouldn't go back, Sadie."

My focus shifted to Ben's office once again, replaying that earth-shattering day in my mind. My lips curled into a sad smile as a tear ran down my cheek. "I wouldn't either."

Way cleared his throat. "It's time," he said, directing us to the church entrance.

I straightened my shoulders, trying to look half as professional as Way. "Let's go."

The three of us strode out of the church and headed for the crosswalk. Way brought his sleeve to his mouth. I heard his voice through the earpiece: "Approaching second location. Driver stand by. Over."

"Ten-four," came Richards's voice.

I scanned the premises, looking for any trap. The Monroes' house was a humble, single-storey bungalow. A tall picket fence enclosed the tidy property, while stubby, snow-speckled shrubs with persistent yellow leaves guarded the front lawn. The area between the beige sides of the house and the fences was fairly narrow; the home's peaked roof sat just inside the fence line. The odds of my family being here were slim, but I wasn't taking that chance.

We climbed two steps onto the porch. A cheery stained-glass window set into the front door greeted us. Way spoke up. "You said there was a Bible study going on?"

"Yes," Pastor Ben responded.

Way put his arm in front of me. "We should stay out here then."

I nodded. Those in the house really didn't need to see the ex-assassin and the FBI agent casually evicting their study group's leader.

The pastor also picked up this fact. "We'll be quick." He disappeared behind the front door. I did not envy the conversation he'd have with his wife.

"Location? Over." Richards's voice crackled through the system.

"In front of subject's home. Over," Way responded.

A chilly breeze brushed the tips of my hair. The neatly trimmed shrubbery by the house rustled. Way stiffened.

A body leapt from the bushes, latching arms around my waist. In a moment, a cord swiftly yanked that body and my body up to the roof. Another masked figure grabbed my wrists and pinned me against the rough shingles.

"Hello, Seamstress."

# CHAPTER
# TWENTY-SIX

Shawn didn't have to take off his mask for me to know it was him.

"Black has been taken. Repeat, Black is taken. Move in!" Way's urgent voice came through the comms. Immediately, his fingers appeared, clinging to the edge of the roof. He swung himself up and reached for his handgun.

"Stop!" I commanded Way. I couldn't see much from my pinned position on the roof, but ticked-off professional assassins were not the type of people to be pulling guns on. Especially when outnumbered.

"We're taking you home," Shawn said. His tone held a hurricane of emotions; he sounded sad, joyful, angry, and worried all at once.

"Where are the others?" I gasped, looking my brother straight in the eye. The mix of pain and determination staring back made maintaining eye contact a brutal endeavour.

"We could ask you the same thing," Dean's voice replied. I twisted to see this brother emerge from the other side of the roof while he gestured to the front of the house. He shook his head at the sound of tires skidding to a halt on the pavement below. "But I don't have to."

Way shifted his weight.

"You really should listen to your accomplice, boy," a third voice from near the chimney said, reinforced by the click of a pistol. "She knows how this works."

Hearing that voice sent goosebumps down my arms. "Hi, Dad," I said evenly, controlling another gasp for air. My brother was not a light man.

The clamour of orders and slamming car doors buzzed through the earpiece. I wondered how much those below could see up here, and whether the FBI had any form of "shoot now, ask later" policy when another agent was threatened.

My stomach tied itself into knots as I realized that now may be my only opportunity.

"Shawn," I croaked, "I have to tell you something."

"Is it a reason for leaving?" Shawn choked slightly on the last word. The grip on my wrists grew tighter and the pressure of my shoulder blades against the textured shingles increased.

"Shawn, it's more than that—"

Shawn interrupted. "Sounds like a story for the drive home." He shifted his weight from my wrists, bringing my arms tightly to my sides and pulling me upward. I countered his motion and flung myself out of his grip.

"No, I need to tell you *now*." I backed up several steps, putting a fair distance between me and each of my relatives.

"We're going home," Dad said as he closed in. Way moved toward me. Dad kept his gun pointed at Way's chest. "Not today, boy."

They weren't listening to anything. That mentality was all too familiar to me.

"Where are the targets?" I radioed.

"Still inside," came the response.

"Get them out now," I replied, shuffling back.

Shawn dived at me, and I launched myself outward from the sloping roof. I ricocheted off the side of the white picket fence onto the ground, propelling myself against what was probably the kitchen window. Pain penetrated my shoulder, reminding me of the still-healing scar I'd gained from my last FBI-related excursion.

Meanwhile, I fervently hoped the Bible study group wasn't meeting anywhere close to said window.

"Where are the targets?" I moved toward the SUVs. We had to get out of here.

"You think we want *them*?" Shawn hopped from the roof, landing between me and my means of escape. He touched the comms unit in his ear. "Mom wants you to come home."

"You're not listening!" I cried in desperate frustration.

"Black, get out of there." The order came through my comms unit.

"Where are they?" I replied, ignoring his directive.

"Black, now!" Way demanded.

I took a few steps back. "Come on, Sadie." Mom's voice came from behind me. I fought the overwhelming urge to turn around.

"Mom, Dad, guys…" I earnestly fought for the right words. I softly finished, "I love you."

I burst forward, leaping against the fence again and pushing off the now-bending structure to hurl my body up and over Shawn's head. His hand snapped up and snatched my ankle.

I screamed as Shawn's muscular arm pulled my body from the air and onto the grass in the front yard. My body bounced as the air fled my lungs. Shawn still gripped my ankle. I spun my body swiftly, twisting Shawn's wrist. His grasp loosened enough for me to slip away. My legs pushed me up and away from my family, while my diaphragm dealt with the impact of the fall. A gunshot rang out somewhere behind me, so I skidded across the pavement for the cover of the open car door. Way was already sitting in the back seat. He reached across the vehicle to drag me into the SUV.

Closing the door, I glanced through the windshield at the rooftop before doubling over for air. One brother was beside Dad, while the other pointed a gun at our vehicle.

Oxygen finally worked its way into my desperate lungs. I fought for another glimpse of my family. My father and brothers disappeared behind the house. In that moment, they were gone.

I looked around the SUV's empty interior. "Where are they?" I wheezed.

Way seemed sheepish. Richards seemed cocky.

I raised my voice. "Where are Ben and Katherine?" I demanded.

"We didn't get them," was Way's timid response.

My fingers combed through my hair as I bit my tongue, fighting the intense urge to verbally tear into the agents sitting in the vehicle.

How could they not get the couple we had come to retrieve?

Why did they leave the innocent in harm's way?

I'd dealt with my family on the rooftop. What were *they* doing?

We sped away, leaving the local FBI agents to clean up the mess that we'd tried to prevent.

Long story short: it was an unbearably quiet plane ride back to headquarters.

# CHAPTER
# TWENTY-SEVEN

I couldn't decide whether I was guilt-ridden or simply angry. Guilt wasn't an emotion that I was horribly accustomed to, so immediate diagnosis was difficult. Logically, both seemed reasonable. Emotionally, they were indistinguishable.

Nevertheless, I was definitely mad.

Way and I dedicated ourselves to filing paperwork. To my huge relief, the hasty escape of the Black family didn't necessitate taking kidnappees, leaving the local FBI branch to retrieve Pastor Ben and Katherine and place them in protective custody.

This eliminated the prime opportunity for the FBI to set up a trap and seize my family, which also was a relief in a few different ways. I had a feeling that my family was as far away as possible, laying low until they could confidently take me out or take me home—whichever was more convenient.

Lovely.

I shook my head to focus on the pages in front of me. This paperwork was my immediate priority. I finished my incident statement, glancing over at Way's. A detail on his document differed from my own.

I cocked an eyebrow. "Richards fired a shot?"

Way peered at me. If he'd had glasses, they would have been perched at the end of his nose, indignantly calling me to be more observant. In my defence, I'd had some other issues weighing on my mind during that moment. The nagging pain in my arm and bruised ribcage attested to this fact.

"When?" I queried in surprise.

"When you ran toward the van," Way said. "If you're gonna look at someone else's report you should read it all and get the context."

"I was there. Didn't think I needed the context," I retorted. Then I pressed. "Where did he shoot?"

"At the man by the chimney."

My jaw dropped. "Did he make contact?"

"Upper leg."

I leaned back and ran my hand through my hair, stretching my aching muscles. Although that shot would not necessarily be lethal, the consequential breaking of arteries and veins in his thigh could have bled out my father's body in a matter of minutes.

"Why?" I asked.

"Why what? Shoot?" Way also seemed to be feeling the guilt and anger of a failed mission. He breathed loudly. "Protection? Ask Richards. Do your paperwork."

I grunted in frustration and clutched my pen. The sooner I finalized my report, the sooner I could hide in my cell, comforting myself with the fact that my family was trained to treat serious wounds. My dad was a fighter. He'd be fine.

Right?

"Oh Jesus, please let him be okay," I pleaded silently.

Way straightened his pages. "Are you done?"

Finish report now. Worry about Dad later.

I stared at my written statement, pushing away all thoughts of Dad's health—or lack thereof—and the whirling emotions that came with it. My report started with the threatening poem and continued until we'd arrived back at HQ. Despite having scratched a few more details in the margins, the report still seemed incomplete. I studied it again. Something just beyond my grasp lingered in the corners of my brain.

I shrugged. "Sure."

"This is hardly a matter of 'sure.' It's yes or no."

"Maybe all I have is a 'sure,'" I mumbled, reviewing the pages again. Way fired one more look at me. "Fine, I think it's fine." I pushed the sheets toward Way, only to immediately pull them back.

"So fine." Way rolled his eyes in sarcasm.

My eyes darted from line to line once more. I placed my hands and their cargo on the edge of the table. "How did we persuade Richards to do this so quickly?"

Way raised an eyebrow. "I've already told you that this whole issue of 'assassin-agent' is odd."

"That doesn't answer my question." Every time Way and I spoke only confirmed that roundabout responses were part of his training, unless he was just naturally that good at avoiding direct answers. Talk about a strange skill.

"Why would I know? I can't figure out Richards's logic." Way rose abruptly and held out his hand for my report. I obliged. "I'll be back," he muttered.

With that, Way left me to arrange my thoughts. Admittedly, convincing Richards had been far too easy. Other facts slowly seeped from my memory. Could what we'd done truly be called persuasion?

I reached for a loose-leaf page and titled it, "Things That Don't Work." I listed the ease of persuasion as the first item. I jotted down Way's comments, organizing them in the order of apparent significance at the bottom of the page. I thought of the shot Richards had taken at my father.

It might have been textbook FBI procedure to shoot, but the timing of it was off. Richards didn't bother to shoot when Dad pulled the gun on Way.

"It doesn't even seem like a necessary shot," I reasoned, tapping the pen against the desk.

Yes, that fact was worth noting. Logically, it all seemed disconnected. In order to make sense of it, one more elusive fact was needed.

The air pressure changed as the door opened. I shook my head. This was far too reminiscent of my "Seamstress" days.

A voice came from the door, but it wasn't Way's. "It's time to call it a night." I turned to see a burly security guard filling the doorframe. I didn't recognize him from past excursions. Way poked his head up behind the guard. Although I couldn't see a clock, I knew it wasn't that late. Way seemed just as perplexed as I did.

I shoved the page in my pocket as I left. Perhaps this was another piece of the mystery.

Time would tell.

# CHAPTER
# TWENTY-EIGHT

I squinted through the darkness at my sheet of paper. Lying on a cot in the near-dark was hardly ideal for such endeavours, but it had grown incredibly late since my hasty departure from Way's office, and I'd worked in worse conditions.

I carefully repositioned myself, shifting my weight between my re-bandaged left arm and my freshly battered right side. My pen touched each written item, attempting to connect the invisible dots:

*Ease of persuasion of Richards regarding my family.*
*Richards's uncalled-for shot at Dad.*
*Ben and Katherine being left in the house by FBI during my confrontation with family, despite imminent kidnap threat.*

I hesitated. The point about the Monroes still churned my stomach, adding substantially to my distrust of the situation. Yes, I'd been the one to put them in danger in the first place, but having them remain in that state needlessly was someone else's choice.

I exhaled heavily, shoving the emotional hybrid of intense frustration and remorse aside. There was nothing I could do about it now, anyway (unless the FBI had a time machine that Way had failed to mention, but I seriously doubted that).

The ballpoint pen's tip continued its journey down my list.

*My work with Way.*
*I'm not in jail or dead; coincidence?*
*Automatically assumed only I could crack the cryptic note on the door; couldn't many other FBI suspects also leave a threat?*

I cocked my head at the last one. Racking my brain, I couldn't remember ever referencing my code name, yet Richards ordered me to interpret the note. Granted, I was highly suspect due to being the only assassin in the building—at least, that was *my* assumption.

Maybe he had more details about my past than I'd thought. It was definitely worth investigating. I ran over the list a couple more times. Another aspect seemed off to me, but I couldn't find adequate language to describe it. Finally, I simply added:

*Way*

~~

"Morning, Way," I smiled as I strode into his office.

Way simply nodded to the egg sandwich on the table. I sat down and dug in. The gooey egg yolk exploded from between the sliced English muffin, sending tasty but messy splatters down my shirt. Thankfully, Way was fully engrossed in his work, allowing me to quickly scoop up the glops of protein without receiving a snarky comment. As the faint spots of yellow yolk disappeared into my black, long-sleeved shirt, I hastily crammed the remaining portion of my meal into my mouth, hoping to prevent further possibilities for embarrassment.

Way glanced up, only to brush my few crumbs off his desk. "You know, I'm not sure I'll miss having to recruit food for you every morning. If I'd only known this came with the case…" Way griped teasingly. I couldn't help but analyze the statement. While it could have been purely passive-aggressive, something told me that there was more to the story.

I finished chewing and gulped. "You sound like you had a choice."

"I did. I could've quit when you were assigned to me," Way quipped back.

Useless.

I changed the subject. "So, what do we have to do today?"

Way used a finger from each hand to compare information between paper and tablet. "You're still technically suspended from paperwork, so you have the privilege of being babysat until Richards responds to our written statements."

"While you try to find my family," I said. The words, dripping with an acid tone, flew from my mouth before I realized that the thought had even crossed my mind. Whether

I liked it or not, a tiny smudge of resentment had buried itself in the darkest corners of my being.

Way returned, "Well, that *is* my job."

I bit my tongue, letting out an agitated sigh. I shoved my hands into the pockets of my jeans, noting that neither of them contained my list from yesterday. I'd somehow missed grabbing the page off my bed.

Way's paperwork shuffled.

All things considered, it was probably better that said list had stayed behind.

Glancing at Way's empty coffee cup, a scheme brewed in my mind.

"Not very often I can see the bottom of your cup," I said, coaxing him ever so slightly.

"Hmmm…Too bad that you're still in custody. I could use a coffee girl," Way replied harshly.

Man, was *he* in a foul mood!

I kept a snide but brilliant remark to myself, allowing a few minutes to pass in silence. Way mindlessly reached for his empty paper cup and brought it to his lips. Frowning in cold and bitter disappointment, he closed his computer window, dimmed the screen on his tablet, and announced grumpily, "I'll be back."

The moment the door closed, I bounced around the desk. A few of Tyson's hacking lessons leapt to memory, and soon I was inside the FBI database. A fleeting thought occurred that this wouldn't help my current reputation in the event that Way or a guard peeked through the door. The next thought assured me that I knew precisely how long Way would take to retrieve his caffeine. The odds of not being caught were in my favour.

Facts flashed across the screen. I typed "Sadie Black" into the search bar. Thirty-six matches listed themselves. Most of them were related to fraud or theft. Two were related to homicide, but as witnesses under protection.

In other words, Richards didn't lie when he said that I wasn't listed at Way's clearance level.

I highlighted the search field and typed in "James Way." As he was an FBI agent, it wasn't difficult to find a match. Nothing surprising there.

I glanced up at the door. The mouse moved to log out of the computer, but hesitated. I swiftly redirected it to the search bar one final time, typing, "Bradley E. Richards." Weeding through the results, I found his profile. The mouse clicked.

The door clicked, too. Agent Way didn't seem awfully impressed.

# CHAPTER TWENTY-NINE

"You know, I'm not sure which surprises me more: the fact that you're on my computer behind my back or the fact that you actually got caught," Way sneered. Only one hand held a coffee cup, leaving the other free to make a series of frustrated hand gestures while he spoke.

This looked pretty bad. Then again, it *was* pretty bad.

Way hustled toward me and signaled for me to move. "What have you really been doing here?" he spat.

"As the one who was supposed to have been thrown into prison, that's what I'd like to know," I countered defensively, trying unsuccessfully to maintain an even tone. I didn't relinquish my place at his computer.

"Really?" Way responded, motioning again for me to leave my incriminating spot. I still didn't move. Way continued loudly, "Well, it's super-convenient that you weren't thrown into prison, isn't it?" Way's words oozed with sarcasm.

"I'd hardly call the last three weeks 'convenient.'" Both the intensity and volume of our conversation were escalating.

"It's more convenient than trying to access confidential FBI files from jail." Way ranted, "Hey, but maybe that's been your plan this whole time! Play the Christian 'I'll turn myself in' card, then—"

"Listen to yourself. That doesn't even make sense," I objected, quickly rising. I was tempted to step onto the chair to look down at him for a change, but decided that it wouldn't be very professional. Nor would it help my cause.

"Makes sense to Agent Martin. After all, you're the one who got me out of the office to hack my computer the day after a violent rendezvous with your family." Way slammed his full cup onto the desk. "I'm such an idiot," he muttered. I felt the steaming coffee spray across my hand.

I finally raised my voice to match his. "If I, Sadie Black, an off-grid, expert assassin, had wanted information from you, I wouldn't have put myself in this position." I could have found a way that included a better shower schedule, at the very least.

"Then *what* were you doing in my seat?" Way dug at me.

"He shot my dad!" I yelled. My voice cracked. A pesky tear threatened to roll down my cheek.

Silence reigned for several moments.

I breathed deeply, lowering the tone of my voice. "Ben and Katherine shouldn't have been left in the house that long. I'm not the only shady character around here."

"Oh, says the criminal to the FBI agent," Way boomed. I inhaled to respond. The phone rang. Way and I both stared, condemning it for its rude and untimely interruption of our argument. He sighed dramatically, glared at me, then snatched up the handset.

"Agent Way here." Way didn't take his eyes off me. Assorted "uh-huhs" and "yessirs" followed, concluded by a "we'll be there." The receiver hit the cradle.

"That was Richards. I'm done babysitting."

~~

Every step toward Richards's office was magnetic, except I was negatively charged, as was his workplace.

In other words, the urge to run the other way was nearly overpowering.

The pressure of the guard's hand against my shoulder reminded me that I wouldn't get far.

When Way reached the door, he wordlessly told the guard to keep me here—outside.

I looked up. I looked down the hall. Panic swept through my body, forcing me to close my eyes and wish I were anywhere else in the world.

"Dear Jesus, I've messed up. Please help me," I prayed earnestly under my breath.

My internal clock echoed in my brain. Five minutes. Six minutes. Eight minutes. How long did it take to tell the simple story of how a manipulative ex-assassin could be re-convicted for hacking into an FBI computer, thereby completely ruining her chances of warning her family about their state of impending doom?

Ten minutes. The guard's breathing behind me was frustratingly consistent. Steady. Almost like it was grounded.

At least someone was.

The doorknob turned, only to stop in mid-rotation. I mustered the little dignity I had left and prepared to be shoved into the unforgiving fire.

Except I could never have actually been ready for whatever was behind that door.

# CHAPTER THIRTY

"Could you please explain what just happened?" I asked, somewhat incredulously, as Way shut the door to his own office.

"What is there to explain? Richards has filed our reports. Your family was not only reported as being at the gala, but they've also threatened an FBI agent, namely me, so now there's a more aggressive search to bring them into custody. You are here because your deal with Richards still stands." Way sat down, turned his computer monitor away from my field of vision and began typing.

"Way. Why am I not in jail?"

He stopped at this and made eye contact. The agent released a slight grin and said, "That's just it, Miss Black. Why are you not in jail?"

I shot him an exasperated look. This game was tiring.

"The reality is that your question has also been my question from the start. If you're truly who you say you are, then the FBI should have locked you up with few questions asked."

Way paused, perhaps waiting for an interjection. He continued: "I'd say both of us were willing to settle for the answer we were given. I, however, would also say that we're done settling."

"And what makes you say that?" I coaxed.

"You got caught using my computer. Risky move. Dumb move. Desperate move." He turned his monitor in my direction. "But it looks like you were on the right track," he said, nodding at the screen glowing with Bradley E. Richards's profile.

"Does this mean you have a plan?" I probed. Would Way ever get to the point?

"Yes. You and I work to dig up what is actually going on concerning this case. Especially concerning him." Way pointed to the screen, reiterating that Richards seemed to be the missing and yet necessary key to answering our shared question.

"On what grounds? You can't keep me here forever," I questioned, testing the vitality of whatever was happening between his ears.

"I wouldn't want to. But we've had two run-ins with your family now. You're our best informant. That's plenty of grounds," he said, hitting a key and reaching for his semi-crumpled paper cup. The printer sprung to life behind Way as the rim touched his lips. His face told me that what was left of his coffee was intolerably cold. He stood and stepped to the door.

I interjected, "So you're dismissing the computer situation?"

"Well, our partnership has already allowed for your use of my office, which technically includes the computer. It's a bit of a grey area, and thus your acts are more of a violation of *trust* than a violation of policy. That's pardonable."

"And this has nothing to do with your chat with Richards before I was invited in?" I pressed.

"It has everything to do with that conversation, Sadie. I'm harvesting information." He pulled open the door, only to close it slightly. "If you're asking if you can trust me, at least trust that we have the same objective. Trust that you can judge me—what's the phrase—by my fruit."

Way met my slight confusion with a sly smirk and motioned toward the office bookshelf. I'd previously noted the various textbooks and binders that lined the wooden shelves, but now I mentally kicked myself for not spotting its newest addition. A thick, grey paperback with a library reference label rested against the other books. Its spine simply read the Holy Bible.

The almost-charmingly cocky agent restated, "I'm harvesting information."

About me.

For the first time in the conversation, I let myself smile back.

"The stuff on the printer mine?" I checked.

Way nodded. "Use the pens on the desk."

Way left, and I grabbed the pages. Bits and pieces of Richards's files were in my hands.

Showtime.

# CHAPTER THIRTY-ONE

Challenges are beautiful things. We bounced between screens and files, searching relentlessly for anything with Richards's name in it. We scoured case files he'd been directly involved with or had commented on, we combed through his background checks for anything of interest, and Way scrolled through years of social media posts on his tablet, gleaning what we could from his private profile.

What we discovered:

Bradley E. Richards had been found by Charlotte Richards, assumed to have been orphaned. They'd guessed his age to be three years old. This lady became his legal guardian, as no documentation on the child could be found.

Charlotte is deceased. Way and I did the math, and Richards was around fifteen years old when she passed, according to the record.

Richards attended the University of the District of Columbia, where he obtained a Bachelor of Arts degree through their Crime, Justice, and Security Studies program.

While in university, Richards was in a bad hit-and-run car accident that nearly took his life.

Richards served as a janitor and then became a security guard at the Smithsonian National Museum of American History in Washington, D.C. as a young adult, with the goal of working his way through his degree.

Richards is divorced with no children. His former spouse was Florence Tanner, who has been employed in the marketing department of People for the Ethical Treatment of Animals. She remarried fourteen years ago to a biology professor at the University of the District of Columbia. They have three children.

Richards joined the FBI in his supposed late twenties. His government employee record shows that he's celebrated two decades of service with the agency.

He's been heavily involved in investigating homicides.

He has two close friends who are used as references. One runs a bar; the other now directs the security department in the aforementioned museum. No one is listed from his childhood.

Based on evidence alone, Bradley E. Richards had no childhood.

Way and I looked over the files again.

"Are you *sure* this is everything?" I hunched over the desk while my fingers drummed my thighs impatiently. We'd gained considerable information but little insight.

"I'm going to run a final search, but I'm pretty sure this is all I can access without referring to the human resources department, which wouldn't release anything due to privacy restrictions." Way tapped briefly at his keyboard, then finished, "But even if they did, I don't know what they'd have on him. The FBI is thorough in its security checks—"

"But it's hard to check a man with no family and few colleagues," I said, finishing Way's sentence. Perhaps it was because of my own background, but I understood that one's family could reveal a lot about a person.

"Wouldn't need to have a big file on Richards anyway. He's been employed federally since university, and he wouldn't be where he is today without a clean service record." Consolidated search results popped up on the screen as he spoke. Way scrolled through the virtual document. "Nothing here that we don't already know."

I sighed. "Can I see?" I rotated the monitor toward me. Way was right; it was the same reiterated information. I sat back, crossing my arms. "Well, what do they have on *you?*"

"Come again?" Way replied, somewhat startled.

"What do they have on you? Like, does the FBI know more about you than it does about Richards?"

Way shook his head. "We are not spending another day's worth of work digging up dirt on me."

I persisted, "That's irrelevant. My point is, you're an FBI agent. Is this type of report normal?"

"Not considering how much time we've put into it," Way answered.

"Interesting," I mumbled, bringing my hand to my chin. My body froze abruptly. "Incredibly interesting." Dots suddenly began connecting; gaps began filling.

"Why?" Way leaned in.

I ignored his question. Showing always beat telling, anyway.

I jumped to my feet. "Time for a walk."

"Can you answer my question?" Way retorted.

I flashed a perfectly mischievous grin at him. "Now you know how it feels. I'll tell you on the way, Way." I reached for the door.

Way grabbed my arm. "Are you sure it's safe for you to leave the building?"

"You have access to disguises. I need to breathe."

# CHAPTER THIRTY-TWO

Today's look was a brunette bob with a jean jacket and a long, floral-patterned skirt. I had also donned a pair of wire-framed glasses and my nose appeared decidedly pointier. Way acquired a T-shirt and jeans for our walk. By the time we hit the street, Way had to work to keep up with my short-legged gait.

"Um, where are we going?" Way questioned.

"Nowhere. Your office is stuffy. Walking stimulates blood flow to the brain."

"Said she to the science major," Way noted impatiently.

"And important things happen when you walk," I concluded.

"Such as?"

I smirked and jumped topics. "How long have we been walking?"

Way opened his mouth to object to my lack of an answer, but a flicker of curiosity bounced across his undisguised facial features. He raised his eyebrows as he answered, "Outside? Three and a half minutes."

"How many police vehicles are on this street?" I probed.

Way glanced briefly. "Two."

"You sure?"

"Well, at least those that are visible. There's a hidden one farther down the avenue we just passed." Way hesitated. "What are you trying to prove?"

"Those were the types of questions that Richards asked me in my second interrogation. Very little about it was personal."

"And?"

"And he showed me the poster of the 'FBI Most Wanted.'"

"Okaaay…" Way dragged out the vowel, clearly perplexed and ready for me to get to the point.

Considering the current situation, I may have enjoyed the feeling of being annoyingly cryptic a bit too much.

"He said I was interesting. Not because of what the FBI knew, but because of what they didn't know."

Way caught on. "At least one of your family members should have been on that list."

"But we never have been. And that, according to Richards, made me interesting. He said there were files concerning the Black family if you had high enough clearance to access them. But that doesn't make sense because my family should have made any FBI list. Clearance or no clearance."

"Yet he knew about you." Way stepped in front of me, walking backwards.

"Exactly."

Way continued, "If the FBI really did know about you, your family would have made the list. You're all too dangerous."

Way swerved to avoid tripping over a fire hydrant. He resumed walking beside me.

"So, the FBI really doesn't know that we exist," I concluded.

"But Richards does."

"Which could explain the shot he took at my dad," I deduced.

Way stopped. "Sadie. I think it would explain a lot more than that."

~~

"Who is this guy?" Way muttered, exasperated.

I cracked open a fresh plastic water bottle, noticing the several empties that testified to just how long we'd been hunched over Way's desk. Having slammed back a mouthful of refreshing liquid, I cross-referenced my handwritten list of people I knew my family had assassinated with the information on Way's tablet. From our research, Richards wasn't close to any of them, nor had he been involved in any of those investigations. Richards had no reason to know about the Black family based on anything we were turning up.

"Someone who is good at hiding things," I said.

"Takes one to know one," Way responded, then continued, "Is it possible that he'd once hired you guys to do something?"

"I suppose. He would have used a different name, which I don't imagine is odd for our—their—clients."

Way wrinkled his forehead. "How do people contact you for jobs anyway? It's not like you can advertise."

I shrugged. "Same way they contact you. They phone."

"Right. And they find out about you through…"

"Strictly word of mouth," I responded.

"In other words, the only way for Richards to know about Sadie Black before you walked through the FBI's door is to have simply heard from someone who's used your family's services, or heard about you and then hired you himself," Way summarized. "But there's no way for us to know that. If either of those possibilities is the case, his tracks are covered."

"And he wouldn't have had the financial ability to hire us until after he'd started working at the FBI, unless that museum job paid really well," I said. "Assassins don't work for pocket change."

"Could have used a student loan," Way mused, turning back to his computer. He jiggled the mouse and began typing.

"But he would have needed that for his schooling, remember? No family, deceased guardian with no recorded life insurance or inheritance…he didn't have anyone to help pay for it," I asserted, reaching for another gulp of water.

"Fair enough," Way sighed. He tilted his head. "I sure wouldn't trust that face."

Way pointed to a new picture on the screen: a college-age Richards. If I hadn't been trained in my profession, I would have dropped the bottle. Grief, I probably would have spewed. Water would have covered everything.

Way caught my shocked gaze. "What is it?"

"He's familiar," I whispered, unable to tear my eyes away from the image.

"Is he a past client?"

"No."

"Does he look like a past victim?" Way pressed. I could practically feel his pulse quicken.

I stared at the determined face on the screen. The resemblance was uncanny.

"No." I shook my head, struggling to piece together the information.

"Who does he look like?" Way fought to keep a quiet tone, despite nearly standing up with anticipation.

"Tyson." I ran my hands through my hair.

Way tilted his head, clearly puzzled. "Who?"

"He looks like my baby brother," I clarified, wincing.

Way compared the picture with my own facial features. "So, you're telling me you think you two are related?"

"It would make sense. The only other way he could know about us is if he'd been born into the Black family line," I explained.

"But who does that make him? What if he just looks like your brother?"

I rubbed my temples, kicking myself for not seeing it before: "That makes Bradley E. Richards…my uncle."

Way still had a look of disbelief stitched across his face. Personally, the pounding in my head and the sinking feeling in my stomach confirmed that my conclusion was correct.

"I guess I should tell you a story."

~~

I'd never met Uncle Gerald. Gerald was the oldest of three siblings, with my dad being the second oldest. My brothers and I didn't know much about him, except that he'd left home when he was eighteen years old. We were told as kids that my grandparents had tracked him down and killed him in Maryland, ending the threat he would have posed to our lives—while sending the same intimidating warning to anyone else who even considered "pulling a Gerald."

I guess he was still alive.

I suppose he'd faked his death.

I imagine he would've made a great assassin.

Everything in our search of FBI records seemed to confirm this. Orphaned Richards—a.k.a. Gerald Black—did not have a birth certificate, just like me. Charlotte likely never existed as his guardian but was only a cover needed to create a believable backstory and obtain the government-issued ID needed to attend university. Richards was recorded as having been in a bad car accident during his college days, which fit into a similar timeline for when eighteen-year-old Gerald left the family and was being hunted down.

Although Dad never really went into detail about the Maryland job, I understood that Uncle Gerald almost evaded my grandfather's shot because of a fluke car accident (which may or may not have been my teenaged father's fault). However, it was possible that Gerald could have used this incident to escape the Black hitlist by appearing to be dead. If this were the case, the damage done to his body may have been enough to alter his appearance or require plastic surgery, meaning that I wouldn't have recognized him even if I'd ever met him. Richards would have had a totally clean slate, with no law enforcement agency knowing about his previous life and no Black family seeking to end it.

That meant Richards could have applied for a job at a federally funded museum such as the Smithsonian, gaining trust until he could graduate university and move into the FBI. It was a career where he could excel and be protected in the process. He'd never have to look back, and in his role, he'd also be among the first agents called if a family of assassins was tipped off, giving him a perfect opportunity for revenge. Gerald being "Bradley E. Richards" made complete sense.

At least to me.

"Listen, I distrust Richards as much as you do, but don't you think you've jumped to one too many conclusions?" Way challenged, even after my incredibly thorough explanation of why this all worked.

"No. I've filled in gaps. I haven't had to jump anywhere," I affirmed confidently.

"But can you prove it? It's not like we can go to his office and say, 'Hey, your ears look like Sadie's ears. You two don't happen to be related, do you?'" Way remarked emphatically. He did pretty well at keeping himself composed, but I could still tell he was going into shock as he processed all of this. As if to confirm my diagnosis, he squeaked, "Did it get colder in here?" as he grabbed his jacket.

"We can do a lot of things. We could search out Charlotte to see if she actually lived and died as the records say, but Richards will not have left a loose end like that. We could run a DNA test—"

"Between you and Richards?" Way interjected. "Family genetics have too many variants to show a clear link between niece and uncle. Not reliable."

"And it would be nice to know before the next encounter with my dad," I said. If Richards were Gerald, the shot he'd taken at my dad would definitely not be his last. "The reality is that we can prove a lot about who Richards *isn't*, but we can't prove who he *is*."

"Thus, we can't prove it. It's your speculation and conclusion," Way asserted.

I shrugged, "It's the best solution we've got."

"Doesn't make it right," Way returned.

Valid point.

"Okay, regardless of who exactly Richards is, we can't trust him to be who he says he is. Too many holes and apparent cover-ups," I said.

Way held up his empty coffee cup. "I'll drink to that."

"And if he is who I suspect, then I don't want him around when I meet my family."

Way folded his hands. "We've got to figure out how we're going to meet your family first. The last encounter wasn't exactly what I'd consider planned."

I nodded. "Let's get to work."

The clock had started.

# CHAPTER THIRTY-THREE

No words could describe just how terribly convenient knowing the Blacks' phone number would have been. With that lovely piece of information, Way and I could have arranged a family reunion within five minutes. The hardest part of our planning would have been figuring out how to leave the meeting alive, or at least how I could get my message out before they tied off their bruised, blue-eyed loose end.

However, leaving alive would be a snap to accomplish if I never achieved an audience with them in the first place.

So, Way and I brainstormed. After looking at our list of ideas, I concluded that we should jump to concocting a plan for actually meeting my family until we could figure out the best way to contact them. Not that the "carrier pigeons" option on our list wasn't an awful one, but it didn't seem horribly effective.

With that, Way and I devised a plan, complete with ways to leave Richards in the dark and in the dust.

Stage One would be to leave the Hoover Building a bit more frequently to dissuade Richards from being suspicious of our absence on the day of the meeting.

Way seemed fairly content to go to the gym rather than sit in his stuffy office anyway. I couldn't really argue either.

Thus, we lifted weights soundlessly, excusing the occasional grunt or gasp. It was a nice change.

Key word: "was."

Way broke the silence. "So how did you train? Like, I imagine you couldn't walk into the community gym."

I placed my pair of dumbbells on the floor, stretching out my stiff side while favouring my left, bullet-pierced appendage. "We built a lot of our own equipment," I said, picking up the weights again. I threw a reminiscent smile into the next set of squats. "And our competitive natures drove most of our training sessions, especially as little kids."

"Why am I not surprised?" Way breathed through a rep, then continued. "I imagine you guys took gym class to the next level."

I chuckled. "You have no idea. My parents…" I trailed off. Did I still have two parents?

I could only pray.

"It was a lot of fun," I finished, pausing to redirect the conversation. "But I imagine that would have been similar to you, based on your dad's occupation."

Way sat up from the bench press. "Ha. Sure."

"What does that mean?" I asked.

"My dad just wasn't super-into 'training me.' I was just expected to know things."

Way turned to face the pull-up bar opposite me. As he reached for the bar, his shirt followed slightly. I caught a glimpse of his back; enough to see marks forever imprinted into his skin.

I may have grown up in a family of criminals, but I'd never been physically beaten.

I let the conversation die. For a moment, I understood the elusive James Way a little better; perhaps that was why Way was so cautious of Richards. He'd seen the abuse of power before.

Way dropped from the pull-up bar and turned to me. "So, why'd you change your mind?"

"Huh?" I questioned as I finished my last set and placed the dumbbells on their rack.

"You didn't want to meet your family. Now you do. If I understand correctly, that has something to do with what you believe, but I can't quite figure out why." Way pulled his arm across his chest, stretching.

I plopped down on the bench and pondered his question. "If I had the cure for cancer, do you think I'd want to withhold that from my family?"

"Likely not," Way responded, switching arms.

"My faith is like that. I believe that Jesus Christ has forgiven me and saved me, so I want my family to have what I have."

Way walked behind me to grab his water bottle. "Then why run away initially?"

"I was scared." I paused and sighed. "I'm still scared that they won't listen and that they'll kill me. I guess the difference now is that I know Jesus Christ is with me and the possibility of them accepting Jesus is more important than the probability that I'll die." My soul ached at this confession, feeling completely ripped out and stripped down, revealed and raw. However, something about my saying it to another human being made it so much more tangible. Solid. True.

Freeing.

I turned to face Way, expecting some form of skepticism or reluctance. Instead, his head was tilted slightly, processing what I had said. The expression on his face was difficult to read. Was that admiration?

"So, you're okay with loving someone who is going to hurt you?" Way asked, seeking clarification.

"Yeah. Yeah, I am," I affirmed. "That's what Jesus has done for me."

Way was pensive as he tossed his almost-empty water bottle from hand to hand. "Sadie, I," the normally confident agent stuttered, "I believe I owe you an apology. I've accused you multiple times of not being who you said you were, but you've made it quite evident that people can—people *do* change."

I picked my jaw up from the floor and blinked several times.

"Thank you for proving me wrong," Way finished. I tried formulating a response, but no words came. Way, seeing my reaction, smirked and added, "Just don't get too used to doing that. We still have a job to do."

Way grabbed his bag and slid into the men's change room. I remained on the bench, still computing the last few minutes of my life. Questions surged throughout my brain, but I had answers for none of them. I guess only God could know what went on in the mind and heart of James Anthony Way.

It didn't take long before we met in the gym foyer and were walking back in full disguise, with a safe distance between us. If we were going to be leaving regularly, then we couldn't always be seen together, nor could we be seen as the same people.

Way walked a short distance behind, allowing for him to still keep an eye on me. He would catch up by the time we hit the FBI building and let me in.

Physical separation also kept me from being distracted by our usual banter. My eyes darted around the landscape, primed to spot any of my family members or other suspicious activity. My nose was engaged for anything familiar or dangerous, and my ears were tuned for sounds beyond the constant noise of the midday crowd.

Just as I walked past a florist's shop, the subtle click of a gun ready to fire echoed faintly from the upcoming alley.

I paused and gawked at the window display, attempting to buy some time. Discounted scarecrows and pumpkins greeted me, accenting the tiger lilies, sunflowers, and bright red gerbera daisies that beamed cheerfully through the glass. The array of fall colours made using the window's reflection as a mirror difficult, leaving me with no way of knowing exactly what was beyond the corner of the stone building.

Way's thin, muscular shadow appeared beside me. Before he could utter a sarcastic quip, I hissed, "Gun in the alley ahead."

I could feel the shift in his body language as he determined his next move.

Way pointed to the dark orange lilies. "Are these related to the deep black orchids you like?"

We'd never talked about flower preferences. Code, however, was a different story.

"I don't think so," I responded. I'd plotted out many scenarios where my family would come for me, but this was not one of them. Granted, I could've been wrong. I kinda hoped I was wrong. It would have simplified our operation tremendously.

A hooded figure slipped around the corner of the alley, a combat knife glistening in his fist and only two nimble steps away. The figure moved swiftly, arcing the blade through the air and into the spot where my shoulder had been only a split-second before. Way reflexively caught his knife-hand at the wrist and used the momentum to twist it painfully behind his back. He shoved the hooded man to the ground, pinned him against it, and tossed the knife at my feet.

If only it were a gun.

I swooped for the blade and crouched against the street-side of the florist shop, only slightly aware of the startled stares from nearby pedestrians. I replayed the sound of our original opponent's handgun, trying to gauge how far down the alley it had been.

My hand touched my ear instinctively.

We had no comms. No backup. No options.

Just a dumb knife.

I glanced across the street. A clear window reflected straight down the alley. A second figure with his hand behind his back was approaching the sidewalk.

I breathed deeply as I scanned the blade in my hand. Scissors may beat paper, but a knife never wins in a gunfight.

A few cars passed, blocking the alley reflection for a moment. When it reappeared, his hand was no longer behind his back.

And I was no longer pressed against the florist shop. Staying low, I darted around the corner and swept his legs. A fired bullet penetrated the asphalt—his balance was compromised but not lost. As he turned back toward me, I sprang up and whipped my foot into his chin. In the same movement, my fist lashed at his hand, sending the gun skipping across the alley. I lunged after it. An arm seized my waist, ceasing the frontward motion.

I grunted as the air rushed from my lungs. My momentum flung me backward into a body, and my hand with the blade swung around to the body's thigh. A deep cry of pain erupted from behind.

The hold released enough for me to push out of it. Pulling the knife back, I spun and my other fist connected with the attacker's face. The now-unhooded stranger collided with the wall and crumpled into the dusty alley.

Sirens sounded in the distance. I rapidly surveyed the site, looking for a third gang member. To my dismay, Way lay unconscious in front of the florist shop, almost exactly where he'd pinned the other guy.

The guy who now bolted toward me.

I crouched, pushing my lower body up just in time to rip his legs uncontrollably from beneath him, sending him face-first into the same wall that his buddy had just become acquainted with.

Blue and red light bounced off the brickwork of the florist shop. I lifted my hands above my head, noting a lady nervously peering from the window with a cellphone in her hand.

I could imagine it was a strange sight: three men knocked unconscious around a short, currently brunette woman panting with exertion.

I didn't want to know what the paperwork would look like for this incident.

# CHAPTER THIRTY-FOUR

The key clanked in its lock. I looked up to see a police officer opening the cell door. He didn't step through but held it open, beckoning me to come out.

Something so simple, yet so annoying—disheartening even.

I shook out my arms as I stood. Was I being questioned again?

Stepping across the threshold, I noticed a second figure in a suit and tie. His arms were crossed in irritation, but something about his posture also said he was relieved I was alive.

"Let's go," Richards said, motioning for me to walk ahead of him.

I didn't move. "Is he dead?"

Richards paused. "No."

I hid my relief at Way's survival and obliged Richards's prior motion.

He and I left the police station and hopped into a waiting FBI vehicle. As we pulled into Hoover Building parkade, Richards said, "Enjoy the view. It'll be a while before you see it again."

"Am I going to prison now?" I asked.

"No," Richards responded. "You just won't be going on more escapades around D.C." He parked the car.

We walked inside the building. "My record?" I inquired.

"Clean."

A security guard met us in the hall. Richards spoke. "Agent Way will be back in two days. I'd like to have a plan in place this week so we can get you on your way." He began to turn away. "Good night, Miss Black."

"Night," I responded aloud, finishing the phrase in my head: "Uncle Gerald."

~~

For the record, I'd spent a lot of time in this cell. Every weekend or day off that Way had—which I learned had been fewer since I'd shown up—gave me a day all to myself. I'd been forced to learn what to do with myself for extended periods of time with only a few clothes, a notebook, a pen, and my Bible. However, no amount of napping, reading, or paper-airplane designing could hasten Way's return quite enough for my liking. Every day that I sat in this cell was one more day that my family was missing out on the knowledge of Jesus.

That thought alone was enough to make me antsy.

Unfortunately, that thought had a gang of other thoughts and ponderings it toted along for company.

The scene from the alley played on repeat in my mind. A part of me was impressed that I'd maintained the strength and the skills to ward off two attackers despite my injuries and a lousy knife. The other part of me only saw Way's comatose frame sprawled across the sidewalk.

He'd been bested by one person. One. Measly. Person. What would happen when he—also someone without Jesus— encountered six more, all trained as I had been and armed with more than a knife and two fists?

At least I had Jesus to look forward to if I didn't survive meeting my family.

On a brighter note, the pain of my beat-up body was easily ignored when I knelt. Sure, my knees grew tired and sore, but the weightlessness that prayer provided made the time frittered between reading, thinking, and experimenting with paper-based aerodynamics bearable. I may have been restless, but I always had someone to take it to.

That was enough for me.

Finally, on the morning of the third day in my rotten FBI tomb, I heard a firm knock. As the door swung back, the light from the hall illuminated a masculine figure holding two objects. A sly smirk pulled at his swollen cheek as he stepped closer and looked me over. I identified the objects as two paper cups from the café down the street.

He spoke. "If you think I look bad, you should have seen the other guy."

I chuckled, thankful that his humour had remained intact. "I did, right before I sent him into the wall. Unless one of the nurses challenged you to a fistfight in the last forty-eight hours."

"Are you kidding? They have way too many nasty sharp things at their disposal. I might be dumb enough to get caught in an alley brawl, but there ain't no way I'm fighting someone who works with needles all day." Way held eye contact for a few more moments.

"Is one of those mine?" I interrupted his trance. As much as I'd rather chat about what happened two days ago, the incessant ticking of my mental clock and the intense urgency to meet up with my family spurred me to bypass that story, at least temporarily.

Way glanced at the coffee in his hands. "I suppose I can share," he said, relinquishing a cup into my welcoming grasp.

"Good. We have work to do."

~~

"Okay, so what's missing in our plan?" Way asked, popping another painkiller and swigging some lukewarm coffee. Although he had several dark, misshapen bruises on his face, his body's defence mechanism of going unconscious had prevented serious brain injury.

"Aside from a means to contact my family, nothing. I can't think of anything else," I responded.

Way sighed. "That's what concerns me." He set the folder on his desk and pulled up a file on his computer screen. "What about this one?" he said, tilting the monitor back to me.

I scanned the displayed data. While the first, physical folder contained the real, our-eyes-only plan to meet and talk with my family, this second, digital folder held the decoy plan to find and arrest my family. Emphasis on "decoy."

"I think Richards will be happy with it," I concluded. "You've done an excellent job."

"Thanks," Way answered, opening his browser's email and copying the document.

A small notification bubble appeared in the screen's corner. The message—really, our hope of stalling—rushed through the internet.

We had four days before the decoy plan was to take place.

Way exhaled, rotating the screen back toward himself. "Now to find those not found before."

I couldn't help but notice his hand incessantly rubbing his temple.

"You sure you're okay to do this?" I asked gently.

Way nodded. "The doc cleared it." His eyes never left the screen.

I rolled mine. The man didn't give up, which was honourable. He also didn't know better.

Regardless, I leaned in. We had a contact to find.

~~

Number of hours we'd spent looking: 17.34

Number of sites Way bookmarked to revisit for future gang busts: 5

Number of times Way left to investigate an old record of potential contacts: 3

Number of times Way left to simply walk and clear his head: 4

Number of times I wished they'd just call us: 14

Number of times we joked about just calling random numbers: 2

"Does this number even exist?" Way grumbled, swiping through information on his tablet.

I reclined in my chair. "It's supposed to. My career would vouch for it."

"Maybe fresh eyes would help," Way suggested.

"No," I asserted. "The deadline's too close. Time to sleep is all I need."

"All right then." Way picked up his cellphone, and I heard a beep from the wireless speaker sitting on his top shelf. Soft instrumental music began playing.

Way nodded to the speaker. "Did you guys at least have one of these in your house?" Way asked, trying to take both our brains off the topic at hand.

"Oh yeah," I began explaining with some level of sincerity. "My brothers wrecked the record player while wrestling, so we had to replace it with something a bit more modern." I paused, awaiting one of Way's usual smart-alecky responses. He blinked twice and dropped his jaw slightly, still trying to sort whether I was actually serious.

Perhaps sarcasm wasn't the kindest means of communication to aim toward the recently concussed.

"I'm kidding," I chuckled. "We had several different stereo systems, although we didn't use them that often. My dad's always been pretty leery of new tech, so we listened to a lot of radio. Kept us informed about the world without being traced to our hole in the ground."

"I see." Way nodded. Concentration was visibly difficult for him, so I didn't blame him…too much.

I smiled, thinking of how my siblings and I would argue over different radio stations. I could practically hear the different jingles of the various broadcasters.

An idea sparked in my brain.

I lunged for the keyboard and began typing furiously. In a matter of moments I was double-clicking a website and smiling widely. "Got it!"

Way jumped toward the computer, reading the contact information for the 1387 AM radio station. Confusion splattered across his face, resolving itself as he leaned closer.

"You really think that will work?" he asked.

"It has to."

# CHAPTER
# THIRTY-FIVE

"Can you please play it a couple of times?" I asked in an older woman's voice. "I really want to make sure my grandson hears it."

A voice on the other end of the phone replied, "Yes, ma'am. We can do that."

"Thank you," I said, shooting a playful, "I told you so" look at the agent across the desk. He rolled his eyes with an impressed smirk on his black-and-blue face. Apparently, he'd never encountered "Grandma Sadie" before—she'd been part of a very effective con back two years ago in Nevada, and old habits die hard.

The radio DJ followed up. "So, just to make sure I have this right, the message is 'Happy Birthday Archer. I would have sent you a letter, but the old post office is out of service. I have always enjoyed your Saturday visits as just you and I watch the sun go down. You are so special to me, and I have so much to tell you. I'm coming to town soon. Lots of love, Grandma Sadie.'"

"Yes, that sounds correct."

"Is there anything else I can help you with, ma'am?" the DJ asked.

"No, I think that's quite enough. Have a good day, son," I said, ending the call on Way's cellphone.

Way held out his personal tablet. On the screen were two plane tickets. We'd decided that leaving D.C. would put more space between Richards and ourselves if he found out, making it less threatening for both ourselves and my family. The only kicker was that Way had now probably figured out the state I'd been raised in.

"You know, I've always wanted to go to Colorado," Way grinned as he tapped his tablet screen and booked our flights.

I remained silent. Way looked up from his technology to see my not-enthusiastic expression.

"What?" he asked, confused.

I exhaled slowly. "Don't you have other things to take care of here?"

"You mean on a weekend? Particularly my weekend off?" Way raised an eyebrow and narrowed his eyes. "Why?"

"Well…" I started, trying to find the right words. "I just don't know that you should go." Way opened his mouth in protest. I beat him to it. "You don't know what my family is like, and you were recently knocked out in a two-on-two match."

"And you want to go out in a six-on-one match? That's dumb, Sadie," Way retorted.

"If we both go and it ends up being any kind of match, then we both lose. If it's just me, I lose and you still have another chance—"

"Another chance to what? Arrest your family?" Way interrupted.

"No!" I exclaimed, only to clarify: "Well, yes, but that's not really—"

Way rose quickly, cutting me off again. "Listen. You're still my case. Your family is still my case. I'm buying two plane tickets. Either we both go, or no one goes. Got it?"

"Fine," I huffed.

Way flicked through some pages and settled back into his chair. "Okay. Let's keep planning."

~~

The haze that covered both ground and sky alerted me to the fact that this was all a dream, but that fact wasn't comforting in the slightest.

Way and I sat on the front step of the old post office. Why we'd chosen to sit in literally the most vulnerable spot possible, I couldn't say. Unlike my memory of the ancient building, this post office was shiny and bright. It acted as a huge target, and we now sat at the bullseye.

Dream Way looked at me and said, "When will they be here?"

"Sunset. Like we arranged," I replied. The rays of the sun seemed dull as they slipped behind the Rockies of Colorado.

"What if…" Way started up again.

"Don't say that," I interrupted. "They'll be here."

I saw the van in the distance, clunking along the highway.

"They're here," I muttered. I closed my eyes and breathed, steeling myself for whatever came next.

When I opened my eyes, I found myself awake in the real world. No matter how many times I'd had that dream, I was never able to finish it.

Even my subconscious mind had no idea how this was going to end, nor was it willing to imagine it.

I got up. It was the day before Way and I were to fly out. We'd listened to the radio DJ read our message, we'd worked out cover and costumes for our departure, and we'd heavily researched the area for the meeting, predicting the hiding places and strategies my family would select.

I still wasn't ready.

I pulled out my Bible to read while waiting for the guard to bring me to Way's office. I flicked to the end of Matthew 28, pleased at the small but growing familiarity I had with the book in front of me. Upon reading and rereading the last few verses, I wiggled back a jacket sleeve and noted the faint, finger-sized bruises that clung to the skin around a battered wrist—marks left by the last encounter with my family. My eyes rode up the arm to where dark leather covered the light bandage and deep red scab from the guard's bullet. The ache in my side reminded me of the trauma this temporal frame had undergone since I'd left home.

Since I'd started following Jesus.

I reached for the pen on my bed and lifted it just above the bruises, thinking back to my reading. Finally, the ink touched my skin and inscribed in big block letters, "GO. HE IS WITH YOU ALWAYS."

"Ready?" the security guard muttered gruffly from the door. I quickly shook the sleeve down my arm and swung my legs off the cot.

"Not really," I confessed, glancing down at my wrist one more time. "But I'm okay with that."

With that, the guard whisked me to Way's office. When we arrived, Way's face didn't seem impressed.

"What happened?" I warily asked the agent behind his desk.

"Richards wants to meet us to go over the plan."

"Tell him we can't. We don't have the phone number yet," I said, regurgitating the stalling tactic we'd cleverly built into our scheme.

"I did. He said it didn't matter. He wants us in his office…" Way paused again, checking his watch, "in five minutes."

I froze. "You think he knows?"

Way pushed himself from his chair. "With as long as he's been in the business, it wouldn't surprise me."

"Smart, Richards," I muttered. We had no time to make a plan to disguise our own. We barely had time to refresh ourselves on exactly what the decoy plan was.

Way, however, had a few-minute advantage on figuring out our next step. "Any thoughts?" I inquired.

"Just follow my lead."

His exuberance did not translate to confidence on my part. However, perhaps the fact that Way was so good at dancing around answering questions would be a genuine asset.

We knocked on the door to Richards's office. Way straightened his tie and flashed a salesman smile at me. My involuntary reaction of rolling my eyes occurred, hiding the fact that, of all the times we'd stood outside this door, this one held the most weight.

Richards sat at his desk, consuming what was left of a breakfast burrito. Bags under his eyes told me it had been a late night for him.

We went over the plan, discussing every point. Richards seemed satisfied. Way seemed cocky. I felt cold; my inner assassin pushed any and all emotion from my body.

"So, this seems in order." Richards finally closed the file. "But how do you intend on connecting with the Blacks?"

Way piped up before I had the chance. "Well, sir, that's all in the plan…."

"No. I meant with locating the phone number to hire them," Richards clarified impatiently.

Way's brief hesitation in answering allowed me to slip in. "We're working on it. I was never trusted with that information."

Richards smirked. "That's what I thought. I've been looking into finding this number ever since you sent your plan." He slid a page across the table. Ten digits in crisp blue handwriting taunted me.

"You're kidding," I breathed.

Richards shook his head. I faked a look of awe. Inside, I continued to push away feelings of anger, discouragement, and fear.

Thankfully, Way was back on the ball. "That's excellent," he said. "We'll add that to today's list. We had some other details to confirm, including this one."

Richards obstinately shoved the phone toward me. "Let's take care of this right now."

"Wouldn't it be better if Way made the call? They'll recognize—"

Richards interrupted. "Actually, that was the other part of the plan I didn't like. They could say no, given recent circumstances involving Way or me. You, Miss Black, hold some collateral."

At that moment, I was ninety-nine per cent sure that informants were not typically placed in such positions. A sideways glance at Way confirmed this.

My eyes dropped to the phone. I fought the urge to look back up at Richards, knowing that could only solidify his suspicions.

I picked it up calmly. I dialed the number.

Ring.

Ring.

Ring.

Click.

"Good morning." A deep voice resonated in my ear. I had never cried at the sound of my father speaking. Today wasn't a good day to start.

I swallowed the emotion. "Good morning, Mr. Archer."

"I'm sorry. You must have the wrong numb—"

"Um, I don't believe I do. This is the Seamstress, and I have your order ready."

Silence. I allowed my meaning to sink in before continuing. "Are you back in D.C. anytime soon?"

"We weren't planning on it. It's really too bad you don't deliver."

I sighed. "It is, Mr. Archer." The perfect scheme flickered to life in my mind. "And I would have sent the order in the mail, but the old post office is out of service."

At this, I heard a voice slightly farther away say, "Sounds familiar." Tyson must have been listening over Dad's shoulder.

"Anyway, concerning the order…I plan to be at the National Building Museum at 3 o'clock on Monday for pickup."

"We can make that work," Dad confirmed.

Tyson's voice came through again. "Hey Dad, do we still have a commitment on Saturday?" The question may have been directed to Dad, but it was definitely meant for me.

"I believe we do, son," Dad said.

"As surely as the sun sets, I'll see you soon. Thank you for your time, Mr. Archer."

Oh, how badly I wanted to add, "I love you."

I hung up and slid the phone back to Richards. His eyebrows creased as he muttered, "Interesting phraseology."

I shrugged casually. "Every family has its quirks," I said. We held eye contact.

Finally, Richards leaned back in his chair. "It's all set then. I'll ensure we have who we need on-site that day. Agent Way, enjoy your weekend. I'll consult Miss Black as needed."

"I will, sir," Way said. He ushered me out of the office and down the hall a few steps.

"Good job," he whispered, lightly hitting my shoulder.

I turned to shoot Way a dirty look. Surprisingly, a look of genuineness gleamed back at me.

Way continued. "Seriously. You handled all that very well."

"He's suspicious," I retorted.

"He was before. I don't think you made anything worse."

I rolled my eyes. "As the sun sets," I murmured.

Way reached for the door to his office. "For many people, that could mean 'I love you.'"

Holding the door open, Way made distinct eye contact with me. The world froze, except for a tiny smile that pulled at the edges of my lips, caused by both the encouraging words and his gesture of holding the door.

"Well, thank you, Way," I said, proceeding into the office.

"Call me James." Way closed the door behind him. "I've never liked my last name."

I paused at the chair, digesting the last four minutes of my life and comparing them to the very first meeting we'd had. I stifled a laugh.

Flopping into my seat, I asked, "So what else do we have to do?"

Way moved around the desk and picked up a packed leather briefcase.

"Enjoy the weekend."

# CHAPTER THIRTY-SIX

Our plane landed in Colorado at 2:04 p.m. Despite the fun I could've had spotting several different security systems in the airport terminal, or picking out suspicious baggage in the claims area, I hadn't the slightest concern for the scenery.

We stopped by the public washrooms to change our appearance for the fourth time during our trip. Way had assured me the agency wouldn't miss a couple of costumes. I hoped he was right, because I couldn't confirm that either one of us would be alive to return them.

Despite the plush interior in our rental vehicle, the three-hour drive to the rendezvous point was brutal. Way tried repeatedly to break the silence, making snide comments about the heated seats or the rolling terrain, but the tone in his voice spoke to his uncertainty. He never suggested turning back, however.

I think he knew I'd get out and walk before turning around.

The old post office looked closer to how I'd remembered it than how my dream had depicted it. The brickwork was aged, the signs were outdated, and the concrete slab surrounding the building posed a serious tripping hazard. However, it was a beloved place in the community and the safest location for meeting my family.

The sun hovered above the mountainous horizon. Way—er, James—and I occupied very different positions: I leaned against the red brick of the post office, protecting my back. James remained in the rental car parked just down the street, camouflaged by the few worn retail buildings and a bare tree.

I pulled off a blonde bob wig, running my fingers through my short hair to the invisible comms unit in my ear. We had no intention of using it.

Then again, we had no inclination of what would happen.

I touched my wrist, visualizing the battle cry that I'd scrawled there.

"You are with me always," I whispered.

A van appeared on the horizon. I flicked my wrist, performing the hand sign James and I had previously decided upon.

It wasn't them.

We continued waiting. I didn't want to think about what would happen if they didn't show up.

I also didn't particularly want to think about what would happen when they did show up.

The sun crept closer to the ground, shooting out a few more beautiful rays of golden light. A brisk, late-autumn breeze swept around the post office, dragging ugly brown leaves along with it.

"Come on," I spoke, rubbing my chilled hands against my sleeves.

Arms locked around my waist and throat, pulling me from my position against the exterior wall. I grunted, reflexively throwing my weight to evade the hold.

Jonathan countered my motion and chuckled. "Getting stiff, sis." He squeezed his already firm grip a little tighter. "Ready to come home?" Hurt and optimism fused in his voice.

I gasped, "That's not what this is about."

"It could be," Shawn's voice came through my earpiece.

"I have to tell you something," I wheezed. My hands flung by my side as I fought for air. Jonathan loosened his grip around my throat enough for me to breathe semi-normally.

Our van pulled up. Dad jumped out, favouring his leg but not breaking his hard stare. "What's that? We weren't enough for you?"

"No." I shook my head. "Well, yes. But it's different," I clarified. "I'm not Gerald."

Dad took a couple more limping steps. "We don't have to let you talk, Sadie. We can end it all now."

"Or we can take you home." Tyson's voice also penetrated the earpiece.

"Give me two minutes," I negotiated, now wrestling against my brother's grip.

"Why? Will your FBI reinforcements be here by then?"

"I have no reinforcements. Only hope. Only..." I paused, searching for the right word. "Only Jesus." Hindsight made me cringe a little at the phrase, but it was the truest thing I could have said.

"She *has* found a guy," Shawn declared. I'd pinpointed his location to one of three places.

"Jesus isn't just a guy. He's God's Son, but somehow, He's human. It's crazy, I know," I said. Was it eloquent? No. Was I scared?

Oh yes.

"There is no god," Jonathan scoffed. I finally wiggled out of his grasp. Dad pulled a gun from behind him and pointed it at me.

I stared at my father, taking a few cautious steps toward him. "Have any of you ever in your lives known me to be irrational? Listen to me then, when I say that I have lived in fear of dying—just as you have—my entire life. Yet I stand here in front of people who, given the circumstances, would be completely justified by their upbringing in shooting me now."

"And?" my father coaxed.

"And I'm still scared. But I believe that Jesus has saved me from death, because I listen to Him now. What scares me most is that you don't." My voice cracked, and a tear slipped down my cheek.

I heard the passenger door open and close. Mom and Tyson came around the van.

Mom's face was contorted with mingled hurt and concern, reminding me that I'd never cried much at home. Tyson's expression also reflected that this was a rare sight.

"Let me tell you what really happened after the Raleigh job," I said softly.

Mom put her hand on Dad's shoulder. Dad spoke firmly. "At home."

"Here," I returned. "Now." Making eye contact with each of them, I pleaded. "Please?"

Silence reigned for a few moments, interrupted by a crackle in the comms unit.

Tyson's eyes grew as he whipped inside the van. "She lied," his whisper rang through the comms.

The click of a handgun came from somewhere behind me. Another two echoed the first, one from the left and one from the right.

"They aren't with me," I said. Footsteps grew closer. I risked glances toward the sounds. I saw two of Raleigh's bodyguards. Shawn and Dean were held at gunpoint in front of them.

I turned back to my family. "Are there only two?"

Tyson responded through the comms unit. "Three."

"Get out of the van, boy." Richards's voice clearly penetrated the air.

I dared another glance. Richards was not within my peripheral, but I recognized one guard as the man who'd shot me at the gala. My mind pieced together all that had happened during the last two weeks, despite my attention being engaged by the sight of my family held at the wrong end of a gun. One conclusion came:

I wasn't the only criminal Richards had given a second chance to.

I cast a frustrated look down the street, making eye contact with Way. He broke his frozen trance to shake his head and mouth, "I didn't know."

The confusion enveloping James's facial features confirmed his statement.

When I turned my head back toward Dad, he sent me the same look I'd given Way. His weapon was still trained on me. I fought further tears.

Richards moved into my line of vision and ordered sternly, "Hands where I can see them." With two of his sons at gunpoint, Dad reluctantly placed his gun on the pavement. The guards pushed my brothers to stand in front of the van. My family now stood within arm's reach of one another. I could finally see Richards. "You too, Miss Black," he said, waving his gun casually.

Dad analyzed Richards coldly. It was hard to say whether there was any recognition.

Richards's finger played with the trigger. He raised the weapon.

My eyes scanned desperately for some way to stall for time. My family couldn't be killed.

"Step forward, dweeb," Richards ordered.

A moment passed before the shock exploded across Dad's face. "Gerald?"

Richards twisted his face into an evil smile, drawing out the state of confusion for his own amusement.

Dad shook his head. "You're dead."

"Oh, Bart. I'm better than that," Richards grinned. "Kneel."

Dad remained standing, clenching his fists and engaging every trained muscle in his body.

"You're dead," Dad repeated. This time it was a threat, not a fact.

Richards studied his gun briefly, then looked up at Shawn. "Do you know how many shots this thing holds, son?"

Shawn didn't answer.

"Hmm. Haven't you taught your kids anything?" Richards jeered. "They probably don't even know who I am."

"You're hardly an exemplary figure," Dad retorted.

"I'm a good example of something." Richards motioned to his guard allies with their weapons. They pressed in. My family struggled against the urge to group together and become an easier target. The monster that Richards had hidden for so long finally manifested itself fully. "Kneel!" he commanded.

Dad held his stare a moment longer, only to painfully oblige. He lurched down upon one knee, still favouring his leg wound.

I stepped forward. One guard—the jerk who'd shot me once already—turned his gun to face me. An eager, evil smile filled his face.

Revenge.

"You spared me from prison to kill me?" I yelled. Just a few more minutes could save my family's lives.

The Black clan all ripped their attention from Richards to me, eyebrows creased in a further sense of betrayal.

The man with the gun didn't respond.

"Richards!" I screamed.

Richards laughed. He wouldn't be deterred by my questions. He barely gave me a second glance.

It was over.

My eyes darted between the gun and my family. Eternity was just seconds away.

They weren't ready.

I was.

I charged straight at Richards. The guard who was trained on me fired immediately, penetrating my side and my thigh.

I threw my body at Gerald/Richards, grabbing his hand with the weapon and thrusting myself between the gun and my family.

Seven more shots pierced the air.

I collapsed, feeling the wickedly hot metal of the gun barrel in my hand and the hard concrete grinding against my skull. My family's distinctive cries echoed as the shock set in. Way's voice joined the noise. A burning sensation ripped through my core. My lungs heaved and contracted.

Fuzzy images of my family floated above me. I gasped for one more breath. "Jesus gives life," I exhaled, finishing what I'd come to do.

# EPILOGUE

Beep. Beep. Beep.

My heavy eyes strained to open. A tidy mess of tubes and wires connected my broken body to monitors and machines. White walls surrounded me. Immediately, my gut screamed, "Run!" However, upon trying feebly to sit up, my gut quickly told me that I wouldn't be going anywhere. Gauze covered my torso in several places. Memories of hitting the cold pavement flooded my mind. I heard the screaming of my mother as the gunshots echoed. Vague recollections of a final, distant shot drifted through my mind, but I couldn't confirm that my beaten body had endured another bullet.

Movement drew my eyes to the brown reclining chair in the corner of the room. Agent James Way closed yet another gossip magazine. How long had he been here?

"Don't speak," he said gently. I wanted to say something now just out of spite, but the idea of any movement triggered a sharp sensation in my brain. I couldn't move if I wanted to.

James's normally sly face was stained with worry as he approached the hospital bed.

I closed my eyes. Focus was difficult.

"Your family is fine," he said. "All of them." I heard the legs of a chair grate against the floor as he pulled a seat up beside the bed.

I furrowed my eyebrows. Even that hurt.

He answered my non-verbal question. "When you jumped, I shot Richards. He was just faster to the trigger than I was." He paused. Somehow, I could hear his sad smile. He breathed and continued, "Raleigh's guards are in custody."

I smiled as widely as the pain would allow. My family was alive.

They still had time.

The agent coughed, bringing himself back to his role. "Meanwhile, Miss Sadie Black,"—his tone was distinctly more professional than it had just been, yet still riddled with concern—"following seven gunshot wounds to your torso and a serious concussion, you have been officially declared dead."

I groaned. I was not dead. Then again, with the amount of medical care I was receiving, could I really say I was alive?

Way continued. "However, in keeping with your unfortunate demise, I'm happy to announce that your new identity has come through. So, assuming you do indeed survive the next twenty-four hours…" I widened my eyes slightly.

Way smiled softly. "Welcome to the world, Miss Sadie—."

# THE END

Don't miss out on what happens next! Join Cydnie's newsletter at **www.cydnietrenholm.com** to receive updates about Sadie and her sequel (still in development), as well as behind-the-book information, short stories, and other exclusive pieces of Cydnie's writing journey.
See you there!

# ACKNOWLEDGEMENTS

"Render therefore to all their due…honour to whom
honour."
Romans 13:7

A huge thank-you to….

Jesus Christ, for giving me the ability, means, and inspiration to write a book. I would never have imagined that the spark of an idea and a passion for Your truth would have resulted in me writing about assassins. You're so good!

Dad, for hashing out plot points with me for hours and hours (literally) and investing so much of your confidence and love in me.

Mom, for encouraging me when I became overwhelmed and enabling me to focus on my writing.

Jakob, Lucas, and Andreya, our sibling dynamic wiggled its way into my writing without my knowledge—and I'm super grateful for that (and you!)

Grandma and Papa, for pushing me to use my gifts and abilities for Jesus and to always learn more.

Paul Deleske (a.k.a. editor extraordinaire), for going above and beyond to invest not only in Sadie's story but into my writing career.

Wyatt Reader, for reading and giving me an honest critique in BMOB's early stages.

Eliesha, Julie, and AnnaRose, for your encouragement and input as I'd gush about Sadie, Way, and a bunch of other seemingly random names.

SAMUEL! Before reading a sentence of my manuscript, you had complete faith and confidence that this could be a success. Your support has meant so much to me, and I love that you've been by my side as we explore both the real world and my fictitious ones.

Also, thank you Reuben, for breaking up my editing marathon with baby snuggles.

# ABOUT THE AUTHOR

Although she's never shot to kill, Cydnie Trenholm co-owns and is the head writer for Moving Mountains Productions, a film company in Alberta, Canada. Her drive for action-packed and truth-saturated stories is the reason this book is now in your hands.

When she isn't labouring over a plotline or working on a film set, Cydnie can be found writing and performing music, studying God's Word, and raising her family.

Find out more at Cydnie's website at
**www.cydnietrenholm.com** or follow her
**@cydnietrenholm** on Facebook and Instagram.

www.ingramcontent.com/pod-product-compliance
Lightning Source LLC
Chambersburg PA
CBHW030927210726
48290CB00007B/2095